THE WORLD BEFORE THIS ONE

D0096704

THE WORLD BEFORE THIS ONE

A NOVEL TOLD IN LEGEND

RAFE MARTIN

WITH PAPER SCULPTURE BY
CALVIN NICHOLLS

SCHOLASTIC INC.

NEW YORK TORONTO LONDON AUCKLAND SYDNEY

MEXICO CITY NEW DELHI HONG KONG BUENOS AIRES

If you purchased this book without a cover, you should be aware that
this book is stolen property. It was reported as "unsold and destroyed"
to the publisher, and neither the author nor the publisher has received
any payment for this "stripped book."

No part of this publication may be reproduced,
stored in a retrieval system, or transmitted in any form or by any means,
electronic, mechanical, photocopying, recording, or otherwise,
without written permission of the publisher. For information regarding permission,
write to Scholastic Inc., Attention: Permissions Department,
557 Broadway, New York, NY 10012.

ISBN 0-590-37980-1

Text copyright © 2002 by Rafe Martin.
Illustrations copyright © 2002 by Calvin Nicholls. All rights reserved.
Published by Scholastic Inc. SCHOLASTIC, APPLE PAPERBACKS,
the LANTERN LOGO, and associated logos are trademarks
and/or registered trademarks of Scholastic Inc.

Arthur A. Levine Books hardcover edition art directed by Marijka Kostiw
and designed by David Caplan, published by Arthur A. Levine Books,
an imprint of Scholastic Inc., November 2002.

12 11 10 9 8 7 6 5   13 14 15 16/0

Printed in the U.S.A.   40

First paperback printing, August 2005

Calvin Nicholls used archival-quality acid-free paper and permanent adhesive
to create the sculptures pictured on the cover and interior, then photographed
the finished pieces with a large-format camera on transparency film.

The text was set in 12.25-point Sabon.

For our real,

living Storytelling Stone—

the Earth—and all the People

—R. M.

◆　◆　◆

CONTENTS

♦ ♦ ♦

INTRODUCTION

◆ ◆ ◆ Storytelling is arguably the Seneca's most ancient art form. From its beginning, it gave us the stories of our world and how things came to be as they are. Young people often look on in disbelief when I tell them there was a time when there was no television, no radio, no video games, no computer games, nothing. It was up to storytellers, those marvelous spinners of tall tales, to keep us entertained and to keep the community's history.

Around a fire in a bark longhouse, families gathered to listen as words painted pictures in their minds; time before the present was remembered and lived again. Things wondrous and terrifying came into the room and lingered long after the departure of the storyteller. The People carried a memory of how things used to be, how things came to be, thanks to the skillful use of words and expressions a storyteller wove together.

Rafe Martin is one of those amazing storytellers. He has listened carefully to and read extensively the stories that emerge from the Haudenosaunee (Iroquois people). People today, as in the past, love a good story, and it takes a special gift to tell stories well. I've watched the mesmerized faces of children and adults as they listen to a captivating storyteller. What was once a regular occurrence in the dead of winter is now a rare treat anytime.

Film, video, or sound recordings cannot quite match a fire and the human voice in a quiet setting. Then it is up to the storyteller to create his or her magic. Long ago our People were given the gift of language, and with that the world was described in every nuance. Trees, creeks, rivers, lakes, plants, animals, and birds were named. We studied the natural world and the gifts the Creator had provided; we were once keen observers.

In the past we communicated with animals and birds, understanding their languages. Today, it is so difficult for most of us to slow down, sit back, and listen to the bird and animal teachers; we don't hear their lessons. They now wonder why we are so deaf to their warnings and are hardly moved by the beauty of their songs. Human beings are rushing in automobiles to the next appointment, away from the woods and open fields. Isolated in front of the television or computer, we aren't the keen observers we once were. Children from the city fear the open woods; they are afraid of animals. The elders of our Six Nations remind us of our duties in the natural world. The storytellers remind us of the beauty all around us that the Creator has provided.

That gift for retelling a good story is alive in the work that Rafe Martin has put together for this book. He has transformed many stories into one narrative that gives the reader a good feel for Seneca and other Haudenosaunee legends. Enjoy them as I have, and allow yourself to be transported to a different time and place.

PETER JEMISON
Seneca Elder
Victor, New York
March 2002

THE WORLD BEFORE THIS ONE

DANGERS

◆ ◆ ◆

"Run!" screamed Grandmother. "Run, Gaqka!"

Gaqka — Crow — dropped his digging stick and ran. An arrow tore past his ear with a sharp *zzzzzztttt*! He jogged left and leaped a fallen log, a broken branch tearing a red, stinging line along his calf. He hardly noticed, for another arrow cut the leaf over his head. *Zzzzoooottt!* Then he was among the trees, running madly, his heart pounding and leaping in his chest. On he ran, leaping stumps and logs, wildly growing brush, and branches. When he could simply go no farther, he threw himself down beside a decaying log, so softened by time and rot that he could dig his shoulder into it. Pressing himself into the soft wood, he let his heaving chest and tormented heart slow.

The log felt cool against his back. Sunlight filtered down through the branches overhead. Birds called and sang. His heart beat steadily. The fierce pounding of his blood faded to a distant murmur. Far off he heard whoops and shouts as the warriors of his own tribe attacked the raiders. *Kill them!* he thought fiercely. *But save Grandmother! Let her live unharmed.*

Exhausted, Crow drifted into sleep. Strangely, after his fearful escape, he dreamed only of birds and their songs. And of a Voice, old as the hills. The Voice spoke, but he could not understand its language. Still, it comforted him just to hear it.

Crow awoke. Twilight was painting the sky. He rose, brushed earth and wood-rot from his shoulders and hair, then set off back to Grandmother and the village.

At the forest's edge, near where the second arrow had almost struck him, he came upon the dead man. The enemy warrior was lying among the ferns, his broken bow beneath him, the arrows spilled from his quiver. The back of his head was crushed in.

A flint knife lay beside the body. Crow picked it up. The bone handle was carved into the shape of a mink's neck and head. He stuck it into his loincloth cord.

"Your knife is now mine," he said. "You should not have attacked us. Now you are dead." He scooped up the scattered arrows. "These are now mine too." Looking down a last time at the dead warrior, he walked on. The forest grew darker. Birds were settling in the trees. Fires were burning and night falling when he entered the big lodge he shared with Grandmother. Six families had once lived there. He and Grandmother, living all alone now, seemed dwarfed by the space. Ghosts swirled up, chattering and whispering, when the wind blew. Grandmother sat by the fire, rocking back and forth, her jaw set, her face hard.

"Grandmother," he said.

"Gaqka!" she cried, wiping her eyes. "I feared . . . ," she began, rising to her feet and hobbling toward him.

"No, your warning saved me. But I was worried that you . . ."

"No," she answered grimly. "Our warriors came and killed some of the enemy. The others fled. But Dog Star, the good hunter, is dead. That is a loss. And Willow Moon and her daughter were both taken. The old man, Lights Fires, was killed too. And many corn plants were trampled." She sighed. "Soon our men will raid their village in reply." Again she sighed. "Here is corn soup for you."

Crow came to the fire. Grandmother ran her gnarled hand over his shoulders and long black hair, wiping away the wood-rot and dirt that still clung to him. She ladled steaming soup into a bark bowl and held it out to him.

"Oh," said the boy before he took it. "See!" he exclaimed, holding up the knife and the arrows. "I took these from one I found lying dead in the forest. Our warriors took his life. I took these things."

Grandmother set down the soup and examined the knife. "It is a warrior's knife," she said. "A hunter's knife. Grow strong," she added, handing it back to Crow. "Be a strong warrior and good hunter like Ga'no, like Arrow, your father. Then the People will welcome us back again." She looked at the arrows. "We can trade these for food. It is well."

Crow nodded. He took the soup that Grandmother now lifted again, and began to eat. "Why aren't we welcome now?" he asked as he ate.

The old woman was ladling soup for herself. She paused. "The things that happened last year — people . . . some people . . . blame us," she said.

"Us?" exclaimed Crow. "But why?"

"Because we still live," she said, shaking her head in disgust. "They think, 'That boy and his grandmother are evil sorcerers. They suffer as punishment for their deeds. We must not help them or bad luck will fall on us too. Our families will die too.' So they fool themselves. Terrible things can happen to anyone. And they do. I am old and have seen it. Now eat."

Crow ate. His cut leg was sore. Soon a scab would crust it over, and the cut would heal. Outside, the wind rose, murmuring in the trees like a voice whose words he could not grasp. The wind passed through the cracks in the lodge walls, making the fire falter and sway. It had been a hard day, a day like countless others. He finished eating, lay down by the fire, and gripped his new knife. His eyes felt heavy as boulders. He closed them and slept.

MOVING

◆ ◆ ◆

"It is time to leave this lodge," Grandmother said when Crow opened his eyes. It was morning. "I am tired of the stares of our neighbors. We will move to the old lodge at the forest's edge. Fewer eyes will stare at us there. It is smaller and will suit us better. We will go there. In the spring you will be big enough to hunt. But for now" — Grandmother sighed, looking around the empty lodge — "let us gather our things and go."

It was a bad way to start the day. But at least there wasn't much left to gather. The warm heavy bearskin robes had already been traded for meat. The carved spoons and bark boxes and packs had been traded too, as had the good deerskin clothing and the moccasins embroidered with porcupine quills. All that had value was gone. Only the oldest spoons, bark boxes, packs, and baskets, and a few digging sticks and worn clothes of thin deerskin remained, along with a few rattles and warped arrows too long for Crow's arm — his father's arrows. The feathers and flint tips would be useful. There were some bone combs, corn husk mats, a pair of old snowshoes, and pouches of dried corn and sunflower seeds as well. No. Not much at all. And Crow's old moccasins, the ones Mother had made for him, embroidered with the moose hair gotten from a Huron trader, and with dyed porcupine quills. Most of the design was worn off, and they were really too small for his feet now. But they reminded him of the good times that had once been. So he packed them too.

They loaded the heavy packs and lifted an armload of bundles each. Grandmother could only use one arm. She needed the other to lean on her cane. They looked around the lodge. For a moment Crow thought he heard laughter and voices. Then there was only silence and the hungry snuffling of the wind. "Let's go," said Grandmother.

Two married women, the sisters Moons Walking and Willows Talk, were outside scraping deerskins with blades of flint and the leg bones of a deer. Moons Walking's daughter, Flowers Playing, a girl Crow's age, was working beside them. They saw Crow and Grandmother carrying their packs and bundles toward the eaves of the forest. The women clucked their tongues sympathetically. "Too bad the mother and father are gone," said Willows Talk, the older and heavier of the two.

"They were strong," answered Moons Walking, pushing back her hair. "Their lodge was well-stocked."

"Yes," Willows Talk agreed, wiping her brow with her arm. "Too bad they are dead. These two may not survive the winter."

"Too bad," repeated Flowers Playing sadly, watching Crow struggle past. She remembered back to when they used to laugh and play together.

Bear Claw stepped from the longhouse and stood beside the women. The warrior heard their words. "Strong ones live," he said bluntly. "The weak die. Of what use are an old crippled woman and a small, scrawny boy?"

His wife, Moons Walking, paused again, wiped the sweat from her forehead with the back of her hand, and said, "Maybe none." She watched the two sorry figures as they trudged forward, pausing every dozen or so paces to readjust their loads. Then she added, "But time will tell, husband."

Willows Talk pursed her lips and nodded in agreement.

"Let it," Bear Claw scowled. "Let time tell."

Three boys watched Crow and Grandmother. One bent down and picked up a stone. "Dirt-Boy!" he yelled. "Clod of Earth! Rag-Wearer!" Grandmother turned and yelled, "Be quiet!" She glared at them, then hobbled on. Crow hunched his shoulders and walked past. *Thump!* A stone hit his bark-strip pack-basket. Crow staggered. He turned angrily and bent to pick up a stone to hurl in reply.

The basket was too heavy. As he bent down he lost his balance and almost fell. A moth-eaten bearskin robe tumbled from the basket. Then a gourd rattle and two cracked wooden spoons fell out. And his old moccasins. *Chhhhhhhk!* went the rattle. *Clack!* went the spoons. A lean dog ran over, grabbed a moccasin in its teeth, and raced off. "Come back!" yelled Crow, dropping the basket from his shoulders and leaping to his feet. But the dog only ran faster. Crow flung the stone, but the dog had already scooted around the corner of a nearby lodge and was gone.

The three boys pointed, doubling over with laughter. A fourth boy looked on, drawn by the commotion. It was Raccoon, Crow's old friend from the time when he still had friends. Raccoon looked troubled and unhappy. Crow grabbed another rock, a big one, and started forward, but Grandmother held his arm. Then she raised her cane and shouted at the boys, "Maybe I *am* a witch!" Suddenly fearful, the boys looked at one another and ran off. As they raced by, Flowers Playing grabbed a handful of pebbles and with a quick, sideways motion of her wrist flicked them at the running boys. They yelled in surprise and, rubbing their stinging ears, chests, and legs, looked back wide-eyed at Grandmother as they ran on.

Angrily, Crow gathered the robe and offending rattle and spoons and the one remaining moccasin and stuffed them back into the pack. His precious moccasins were separated. That mangy dog was already off somewhere gnawing on one. So things continued to fall apart, and the day that had begun simply bad now turned awful.

Crow slung on the pack-basket and staggered erect. Grandmother lifted her bundles. Then once again they trudged on, neither speaking, and no one speaking to them.

Moons Walking commented, "Something stung those boys."

Willows Talk said, "Bees. Wasps."

"No doubt," answered Moons Walking. "And you? What do you think?" she asked, turning to her daughter.

Flowers Playing looked up, shrugged, and said quizzically, "Maybe bees? Maybe wasps?"

"Hmmmm," said Moons Walking. "Maybe well-aimed bees and well-aimed wasps."

The lodge in which Crow and Grandmother set their things down was small. The roof poles were blackened by smoke. The bark walls were cracked and split. Crow liked it, somehow. Though it was old and burned and broken it held no memories for him — no ghosts — of the happy world that had once been.

"There," said Grandmother, setting her pack down against the bark wall. "We'll sweep out the leaves and dirt, reset the stones in the fire pit, cut a few sticks to hang a clay pot over the fire, and pack our things away. It will be our home."

Crow looked around. The oldness of the place comforted him. It had endured. He nodded.

"Those moccasins," Grandmother said offhandedly, "were too small. That stupid dog did you a favor. Keep the one moccasin that remains, if you like. It will make a pattern, someday, for a new pair that fits."

Crow swallowed and nodded again.

Later, when the old lodge had been swept out, the stones reset, the branches cut, the firewood gathered, and their few belongings stored beneath the sleeping platforms or hung up on the poles, Crow wandered back into the forest. The dead man was gone. The warriors had already come and dragged the body away. A few bloodstains, some mashed and trampled leaves, a line of ants, and a cloud of bugs — these were the only traces of death that remained. In a few days the forest would have entirely reclaimed the spot as its own.

Who cared or remembered what had been?

The wind moved. Ferns swayed and bent. Leaves whispered. Trees groaned and sighed.

I do, he thought, answering his own question. *I will not forget. When all have forgotten, I will remember what has been.*

He shivered. The wind sighed. And on the wind a voice that seemed to whisper, "Thaaaaat's goooooood."

GAQKA, CROW

◆ ◆ ◆

THE wind howled through the cracks in the elm bark walls of the old lodge. Through the late summer and fall and into the depths of winter, Crow and his grandmother lived alone in the small old lodge separated from the cluster of longhouses that sheltered the other families of the People. Twice during the most brutal days of winter's cold they had found deer meat, frozen hard as stone, lying beside the lodge entrance. Another time there were ears of dried corn and a pouch of acorn meal. Another, a sack of sunflower seed. And yet another, an old bearskin robe, frayed and tattered, but with good use still in it. Someone, maybe more than one person, had thought of them. These gifts had helped keep them alive through those bitter days. But other than that, it was as if they no longer existed in the village at all. It was as if they were already dead and forgotten.

The wind blew. The smoke whirled up from the fire in a ball-like

puff and struck fiercely, biting at the boy's nostrils and eyes. It was like an attack by one of the dreaded Rolling Heads — monsters with long blowing hair, big mouths and teeth, but no body or legs — that lurked deep in the woods ready to chase and eat the unwary.

Grandmother pulled the old bearskin robe around her thin shoulders and moved in closer to the fire despite the acrid, stinging smoke. She coughed as the whirling smoke attacked.

The winter had been long and bitterly cold. It might yet prove deadly for an old woman and a boy who had scarcely any food left.

Just last winter they had been warm and well-fed. Father's hunting skills had seen to that. A sudden memory made Crow's mouth water: cornmeal soup, savory with dried corn, potatoes, beans, wild onions, and deer meat bubbling in a pot on the fire; frybread on a bark tray nearby, ready for dipping. His stomach rumbled and ached. In his mind he walked around the old lodge, eating good food, smelling delicious odors, feeling the weight of warm winter robes. The lodge in his mind was always well stocked. Herbs, sunflower seeds, braided corn, dried meat, gourd-and-bark rattles, turtle-shell rattles, bows, lacrosse sticks, snowshoes, and spears — all were there. And tanned hides, embroidered moccasins, bark boxes, clay pots with fluted rims, and carved-bone hair combs too.

A painful image, those bone combs. His mind slowed as he saw again his mother's combs, designs of the heron, her clan symbol, carved into the rim. He saw her hands, those strong workers but always soft, kind friends to him. The dark, bright eyes and long, dark hair of Mother had been mirrored in the small form of Little Sister. When fever took them, not long after Father disappeared while out hunting in the deep snows, it seemed that his own life ended.

The memories faded. He felt the cold again, heard the bitter north wind blow and the snow rasp along the bark walls like a thousand bony fingers — Old Man Winter hungrily prowling, hard at work.

Another image rose now — they came endlessly if he let them, the pace intensified by hunger. A strong face, white teeth, and the sound of laughter over snow. Father was sliding his favorite greased and polished wooden snow-snake down the mile-long groove in the snow. He won! How he laughed! Father.

The image grew thin. He could not hold it. The scene rippled, shredded on a draft of cold wind, and was gone.

Grandmother's dry, rasping cough brought him back to the misery of the present. Grandmother coughed again.

"In the spring," she whispered, each word costing her much effort, "you will be old enough." Her voice fluttered weakly, then gained strength. "Your father, Ga'no, was a great hunter and warrior. If only he had died in battle we might have forced the warriors to steal a slave from among our enemies to serve us. But no one could best him." She sighed. "No matter. You will be like him. You will hunt, and we will eat. Spring is coming. Old Man of the North will be driven away. Young Man Spring will smile. Up from the good south he will come. His breath will melt the rivers. The fish will leap. His hands will warm the trees, and sap will flow. Leaves, blossoms, and fruit will ripen. Green herbs will lift their heads again. The Three Sisters — Corn, Beans, and Squash, the Sustainers of Life — will dance once more above the body of our Mother Earth."

Grandmother paused. When she began again her voice had fallen to a breathy whisper once more. "Rest. Spring is coming. Here." She passed him some dried meat and dried corn flour. "Just a little. Eat slowly. Make it last. Then rest. Rest."

Outside, the north wind howled and moaned like a hungry beast. All else slumbered in the Great Sleep of winter. Crow shivered. He missed Mother and Father. He missed Little Sister. He remembered the days when he ran happily through the village with his friend — Jo-ah-Gah — Raccoon, tossing stones and sticks at imagined prey and foes. Teasing Flowers Playing! The wind moaned again. The cold penetrated the lodge as if seeking out his little precious spark of life. Desperately he thought of spring. Weak and tired, cold, hungry, and lonely, he smiled. He would be a man like Father. He would hunt. Grandmother's words gave him strength.

"Spring is coming," said Grandmother huskily. "Rest. Like your namesake, the Crow, you will find a way through darkness and bring life to what is lost. You are almost old enough. I can feel it. But rest now. Rest."

THE BOW

◆ ◆ ◆

Leaning on her hickory stick, Grandmother hobbled toward Crow. She held a boy-sized bow and a quiver of small arrows in her thin hand, a hand twisted and wound with veins like old roots. Her wrinkled face was alight with pleasure this spring morning. Winter had passed, and they had survived. The air was chill, but the sun was warm. Grandmother's thin lips curved in a smile. "Try your skill with these, Grandson."

Excitedly Crow slung the deerskin quiver of flint-tipped, red-willow arrows over his shoulder. He tested the draw of the hickory bow, feeling the resisting pull of the sinew bowstring. He slid an arrow from his new quiver, set it to the bowstring, and drew the string back until the feathered nock lay against his cheek. "That . . . pinecone . . . Grandmother," he panted, for the draw of the bow took all his strength to hold.

And he let his arrow fly. *Zzzzzzzzzt!* It struck the pinecone solidly, knocking it to the ground.

Grandmother slapped her thigh. "*He-dah!* I knew it!" she sang. "You have the power! Not for nothing was your father given the name 'Arrow.' You have his skill. Listen! It was he who aged and shaped this bow for you and he who chipped the arrowheads. You will be a great hunter, just as he was! Shoot again!"

Crow retrieved his arrow, set it to the string, and bent the bow. His shoulders shook. "That . . . dead branch . . . Grandmother!"

He shot. The arrow struck, snapping the branch from the tree with a loud *crack!*

"Ahhh!" nodded Grandmother approvingly. "A fine shot! We will eat soon!"

Four times in all, Crow shot, and each time he hit exactly where he aimed.

"Birds, little Gaqka," laughed Grandmother excitedly. "Go now! Hunt birds!"

Crow set off. When he stepped from the clearing and walked among the trees he felt like he was already a man. He was on his own, alone in the forest, the domain of men, far from the women's fields. He had his own bow. He would bring home meat. So what if those he fed were only Grandmother and himself? So what if the meat he brought were only birds? Her fate and his were in his hands.

Everywhere he looked life was returning. Mushrooms sprouted on rotted logs. From the forest floor, wet with new-melted snow and clotted with dead, sodden leaves, bright flowers — snow-drops — were rising. New leaves, small as a squirrel's foot, were unfolding on the branches above. The wind rushing through the forest made a soft *whooooshing* sound. Water ran gurgling down from the surrounding hills.

At day's end, Crow returned tired and happy, a string of birds over his shoulder. "We shall eat well!" exclaimed Grandmother. "Eat?!" she cried scornfully. "What do I say? We shall feast! And we will have bone-splinter needles with which to sew clothing. We will have feathers for arrows, and down for warmth. This is what a man does!"

Crow glowed, warmed by her praise. He recalled the times Father had returned with a deer or turkey or even bear, and how food, clothing, tools, and weapons had all come from its body. Now he too was becoming a man.

He unstrung his bow and placed it by his reed-mat. He slung the quiver on a post that rose to the smoke-blackened bark ceiling high above. Grandmother gutted and cleaned the birds swiftly with skilled hands. Soon, the old, drafty lodge with its cracked walls and roof filled with the good smells of roasting meat and the sizzle of fat and grease dripping into the fire.

That night, Grandmother and Crow ate well. Then they happily licked their fingers, lay down, and slept soundly, their bellies full at last. And when those birds were gone, Crow hunted again and always brought back more.

Spring passed swiftly and happily. The Sugar Moon passed, and the Planting Moon arrived, followed by the Strawberry Moon of early summer, with its refreshing red berry juice to drink. The warm, seventh moon followed, the Blueberry Moon. The Sisters, Squash and Corn and Beans, ripened. The full, shimmering, stifling heat of the Green Corn Moon arrived. Blackberries, puffballs, and pond lilies were gathered and eaten. Then the Moon of Freshness rose, bringing its cool relief. Soon, so soon it seemed to come, the Moon of Falling Leaves was again new. Crow and Grandmother's stores of dried corn and sunflower seeds were almost gone. But the sunflowers were heavy and nodding on their tough stalks, the heads full of dark seed, and the corn was standing tall. And there were birds, always birds to eat. Life was good. The bow, and Crow's skill with it, had restored them. He was a man. Or almost a man. Grandmother said so.

One early fall day, Crow was sitting beside the fire, straightening his arrows. He warmed each shaft, then drew it through a notched stone, sighting down along its length. When he was satisfied that it was again properly trued, he laid that arrow aside and lifted another. As he worked he thought, *Soon these arrows will find the swift rabbit's heart. Then raccoon, turkey, and beaver will fall. By the next Planting Moon I will be strong enough to stalk the deer. The People will begin to notice. Then the great day will come. I will* bring Grandmother the sweet meat of old Shaggy Paw. *The People will call out, vying with one another for my attention. "Come," one will shout, "enter our lodge." "No, enter ours!" will exclaim another. "We did not know your power. We never would have been so cruel if we had known!" And I will say, "It is nothing. I can feed you all. I have Father's power."* He sighed happily. The future unrolled before him as effortlessly as a boulder rolling and bouncing down a hill. The bow had opened the way. His strength and skill would increase. Good times lay ahead, no longer forever behind, locked in the storerooms of memory. The trail ahead was well-marked and clear. All he had to do now was follow.

THE ROCK

♦ ♦ ♦

CROW strolled through the sunlit forest, nibbling distractedly from a pouch of parched corn, a string of birds dangling over his shoulder. He was deep in the forest, among the big trees and clumps of fern, when he noticed that a feather on his arrow had come loose. Looking for a place to sit and retie it, he spied a boulder rising from among the underbrush in a clearing ahead. He headed for it.

Soon Crow was seated comfortably on the great, round, gray, moss-covered stone. He drew a length of sinew from a small deerskin pouch, chewed it till it was soft, and retied the loosened feather. He was sighting along the arrow-shaft, making sure that the feather was properly aligned, when a deep, calm, patient, old voice said, "Would you like some *gaga'sho^n'o*? Would you?"

Crow dropped his arrow with a clatter. Heart pounding, he

looked all around. But no one was there! He grabbed his fallen arrow, set it to his bow, and stood up on the stone, alert for danger.

Again, the deep old voice spoke, saying this time, "It is courteous to answer a question when someone asks. So, would you like to hear *gaga'sho^n'o*? Would you like some Long-Ago Time stories?"

"Who are you?" stammered Crow. "Where are you? What do you want? Show yourself!"

"Show myself?" chuckled the Voice. "Oh, that I did, long ago. As to who or what I am, I am just an old piece of turtle shell. But I am awake. And I know stories. What do I want? To tell them. As to where I am — why, you silly two-legged, just look down."

Crow looked. Aiiiiiiiiiii! It was the stone! The *Voice* came from the stone! Crow dropped his bow and arrow and scrambled off the boulder in such a mad rush that he landed in a tangle among the ferns.

"Ho, ho, ho," laughed the Stone. "You are quick! But why be afraid? I have no mouth with which to gobble you up. Be at peace. Just tell me, do you want to hear Long-Ago Time stories?"

"What are . . . Long-Ago Time stories?" stammered the boy as he untangled his arms and legs, pushed back his long black hair, and rose bravely to his feet.

"They are the tellings of things that happened long, long ago," answered the Stone, "in the world before this one."

"If that is what they are, then, yes, I would like to hear them."

"Leave your weapons. Let them lie there," said the Stone.

"Climb back up and seat yourself. Good. Now, give me a gift. Hmmm. Those birds will do. If you give gifts, I will tell stories."

So Crow placed the string of birds upon the Stone.

"Now, listen," said the Stone, "for long, long ago, in the world before this one, it was like this:

There were seven brothers. They were young, but men's hearts already beat in them. Together they trained as warriors, together they danced before their lodge, keeping time on a little drum. But their mother was restless and wary. She took no joy in their dance or in their warrior skills. In truth, she had little desire to see them leave her and test themselves in the wide world.

One day, as the boys danced, they felt the power growing in them. Their movements were perfect; their feet seemed to fly tirelessly over the earth. Then they went excitedly to their mother and said, "Mother, give us parched corn and corn cakes and other foods such as warriors take when they travel. It is time we went out into the world to test our courage and skill. The time has come."

But their mother answered, "Oh, do not go yet. I have nothing proper for you to eat. Wait yet another season."

The boys insisted. "Mother," they said, "give us what we need so we may journey like men."

But again she said, "Truly I have nothing to give you now, so do not go."

Then the boys began to dance once more. And again, the power of the dance came on them. Their feet flew tirelessly. Their movements gave them strength. They looked at one another and said, "Surely it is time. We are ready."

And again they went to their mother to ask for food for the journey. But again she refused them, wanting them only to stay.

"Now," said the eldest, "we must dance and show our power."

The boys danced. Their feet flew. Strength flowed into their legs. Their hearts grew light.

This time their mother too felt the power of the dance. The drumming and singing made her hair stand on end. Out she rushed from the lodge. There were her boys, dancing and singing. But they were dancing and singing and circling in the air! Higher and higher they rose, dancing all the while. The mother screamed, "Come back! Do not go! Return!"

But on they sang and on they danced as higher and higher they rose. Now they were at the top of the lodge pole, now above the trees. Up and up rose the boys, dancing and singing. Now their voices came down like whispers, they were so high. Now they seemed like tiny specks high up in the sky.

"Come back," cried the mother, "return!" Way high up, the dancing boys heard her voice faintly calling. And they felt the tug of her concern and loss.

"Do not look back!" insisted the eldest. "Keep dancing! We are up high. Do not falter!" But one did look down. He saw now how high they had risen. His mother's tear-streaked face, so far away, seemed to fly up toward him. Her outstretched arms reached for him. He turned and reached back. He fell. Like a bright streak across the sky he went. Down.

Then only the whispering trees remained, echoing her anguished cries, fluttering and whispering in the wind. The other boys were gone.

The mother ran to where the one had fallen to Earth. From the spot rose the first white pine tree, tiny still but clearly growing. That is the tree that when cut bleeds reddish sap, like blood. That night the woman looked up. Six new stars sparkled close together in the skies as if moving and dancing.

The six brothers had journeyed to the heavens. Look up. They can be seen on clear nights after the first frost. Sometimes six stars seem to dance, sometimes seven. When they shine overhead, it is midwinter, a good time for people to share dreams, dance and feast.

Is that one's fall a warning? Some might say, "Yes. One must be strong. Never look back!" Yet from that fall came the white pine.

"So it goes," said the Stone, "the story of the Dancing Boys. And the shaping of our world. Did you like it?"

"Oh, yes," Crow whispered, almost despite himself.

"Hmmmm," murmured the Stone, pleased. "That is good. You listened well. Shall I tell another story?"

"Yes!"

"Listen carefully, then," said the Boulder, "for this one is very old, much older than the first. Many things — failures and triumphs both — have made our world as it is today. But long, long ago, way way back, in the world before this one, it was like this.

There was no earth, no light at all, only water. High up, in the Above World, Sky People lived. Their world could travel. It had a thin crust, and the chief's wishes could make it go wherever he desired. In the center of the Sky World was a tree. Bright fruits of all sorts hung from its branches, and there were buds and leaves and fruits and seeds, all at the same time. The perfume from that tree filled that world with a delicious aroma. Four roots ran from the tree, one in each direction — north, east, south, and west. At the tree's top was a great blossom of light, illuminating the whole Sky World.

The chief of the Sky World had recently married a young and beautiful maiden, and they were happy. One night the chief dreamed that the great tree of light must be uprooted and that what was below its roots must be seen. His wife cautioned, "Maybe sorrow and trouble will come of this." But he was determined. Gripping the tree, he struggled mightily. Then, with a great *rrriiiiiip*, the roots snapped, and the entire tree pulled loose. Many leaves, fruits, seeds, and buds shook down from the tree and lay scattered on the ground all around the gaping hole in the Sky World's crust. The chief peered down. It was dark. He could see nothing. His wife approached and peered down too. Suddenly she slipped and fell. She grabbed desperately at the ground around the hole, seeking to hold tight and stay her fall. But only seeds, buds, blossoms, and broken bits of root filled her hands. Then down she fell, tumbling down down into the whirling darkness below, and was gone from sight.

She fell through whirling clouds, her long hair streaming in the wind. Oh, Sky Woman fell and fell. For a long time there was only falling.

Then, far down below, ducks and geese resting on the endless waters saw something coming down. They saw Sky Woman and they lifted their wings and rose to meet her, saying, "We will cushion her fall!" With their wings and feathered backs they made a soft resting place, and on it they carried the woman from Above safely down toward the dark sea. Then a huge turtle rose from beneath the surging waves, and they gently set Sky Woman down on Turtle's back.

"We need earth to cover this shell," they said. A duck dove. Down down into darkness, colder and farther and deeper. Then Duck bobbed back to the surface, exhausted. He had not touched bottom. A goose tried. Down and down and down she dove farther and farther. She too gasped her way back to the surface. She had not touched bottom. A pike swished its tail, pointed its nose, and plunged down. Its eyes bulged in the dark water. It could not reach bottom. Then Muskrat said, "I will try." She took a deep breath and dove. Down and down and down and down and down she plummeted into the dark dark sea. Bubbles streamed from her nose in a thin, silver trail. She bumped something down in the cold and dark. She turned and swam up up and up. Struggling up from deep deep down in the dark water. On her nose was a smear of wet earth.

Then the ducks and geese spread the earth over Turtle's shell. And the shell grew and grew and grew as they spread that tiny bit of earth, until there was a world for Sky Woman. Seeds carried from the Sky World dropped from the woman's tired fingers; bits of root and bark and broken buds scattered and fell. And from the seeds and roots and blossoms, grass and trees and bushes and herbs sprang up. A world, this world, took form. At the top of a tall tree shone a bright blossom. Now there was light.

The woman walked all around her new home. She felt a stirring within her. She lay down in the grasses. Her daughter was born.

Sky Woman and her daughter lived happily. They had all they needed. Her daughter became a young woman. On the breeze someone came to her. A spirit and a man. It was Wind. Soon the daughter felt life stirring within her.

Sky Woman said, "Again something will happen, something new will happen again."

Two children spoke from the daughter's womb. One's voice was gentle, the other's hard. The soft-voiced was born first. Then came the one whose voice was hard as flint. He kicked his way out through his mother's side. The daughter of Sky Woman died. She was the first. She took the path that returned to the Sky World, where her father waited to receive her home.

But her body was buried in the earth. And from the head of the grave rose a sacred tobacco plant, an herb whose smoke carries prayers back to the Sky World. From the area of her heart sprouted the first corn. From lower, over the belly, grew squash. And from the foot of the grave sprouted potatoes. These, the final gifts of the daughter of Sky Woman, are precious. Cherish them.

Now Sky Woman raised her grandchildren. Those boys had power. They created things, but their minds were different. Good-Minded created rivers that flowed up- and downstream on each side of the bank. "Someday people will travel easily on these rivers, up- or downstream, wherever they want to go," said Good-Minded. Hard-Minded changed that so the rivers flowed only in one direction. "Let people work hard to get where they want to go," he said. Then he put rocks and boulders in the rivers and he laughed. Good-Minded made new trees — apple and beech and oak and willow and chestnut. Hard-Minded made thorny briars, poison ivy and oak, nettles, thorns, and burrs. Good-Minded put fish in the rivers — salmon and trout and bass. Hard-Minded threw many little sharp bones into the fish and then made lampreys and leeches. Good-Minded made the animals — panther and wolf, bear, deer, and moose, squirrel, raccoon, bobcat, beaver, otter, and lynx.

Hard-Minded trapped many of the animals and made them fierce, made them want to hunt other animals and kill. Then he made rattlesnakes and copperheads, ticks and spiders. Good-Minded made the beautiful birds and good insects — bees and ants, butterflies and dragonflies. "*Buzzzzzzzz*," sneered Hard-Minded, who formed swarms of mosquitos, gnats, hornets, and flies. Then he ran off to do mischief, making stony places, and steep cliffs, and rocky ways.

Sky Woman said, "It is time for me to go home now. To take the Sky Road and return. There is one thing more to do, though, before I leave." She took flakes of mica and little shiny rocks and tossed them up into the sky. They stuck there, glittering. "Stars." She laughed. "Look at them shine!" Then Sky Woman was gone.

Good-Minded looked into a pool of clear water and saw his own face. Then from wet earth he made men and women. "You look like me," he told them. "You too are descended from Sky Woman, for my breath is in you. This earth is yours. Be friends to one another, help one another. You are all related. Offer prayers for the animals you take as food. Cherish the growing things."

"From these first people all people today are descended," said the Boulder. "Even those you call 'enemies.' All this took place long ago. So many things have happened since then, it would be impossible to say it all. The story of the world is very old and strange. Things you could not even yet dream have already happened. Let us stop for today," concluded the Boulder. "But come back tomorrow. Bring gifts and I will tell more stories. But tell no one. For now I speak only to you."

"But," exclaimed the boy, shaking his head and running his hand through his long hair as if to untangle his jumbled thoughts, "how could the ducks and geese and muskrat and pike be there before Good-Minded created animals? And where are Good-Minded and Hard-Minded now? And when people die, do they all take the Sky Road and go to the Sky World? And was it just chance that Sky Woman fell? Is our world just the result of a slip? Or was it destined and meant to be? And —"

"Slowly," chuckled the Stone. "Patience. You ask good questions. But I have a turtle-shell mind. My way is slow and steady. Come back tomorrow. I will answer your questions and tell more stories."

"I will return," said the boy with an impatient sigh. Then he took up his arrows, bow, and knife and slid from the Rock. "Farewell," he said.

But the Rock was silent, as if it had never spoken at all.

Crow headed home. The sun was low among the trees, and a deep, reddish glow spread across the leaves. The old, familiar world seemed strange to him now. Had a rock really spoken? A few birds twittered and flew. He shot them and tied them to his carrying string.

It was twilight when he stepped from beneath the trees. Grandmother's anxious voice was calling, "Gaqka! Croooooooow!"

"Here, Grandmother!" he called.

"At last!" she exclaimed. Grandmother was standing at the lodge entrance, leaning on her cane. Her figure seemed so frail against the firelight, like a shadow or mist the wind might whirl away. "You have been gone a long time," she said, peering anxiously at Crow as he approached. "Enemies prowl. You know the danger. Why did you not return while it was still light?"

"I have been . . . hunting, Grandmother," he answered. "See. Here are birds."

She took the string. Three small birds dangled on it. "But you have been gone all day, Grandson!" she exclaimed, disappointed.

"I had to travel far to find these," he answered. "But I will hunt tomorrow. I will bring us food."

"Let us eat," sighed Grandmother.

Later that night Crow lay on his mat and listened to the wind rustling the leaves. A chill breeze blew in, whirling the ashes and brightening the embers of the fire. North Wind, Old Man Winter's helper, was blowing. The Harvest Moon had come. *Hunting will soon become harder,* Crow thought. *We need to dry and store winter foods. The Hunter's Moon and the Cold Moon will come quickly now. I will not let Grandmother down. I will not betray her trust.*

But in his mind a large round shape loomed from the shadows. Voices spilled endlessly from it, pouring down like rainwater. He strained to make out the words, but the voices overlapped, spoke in languages he did not know, so that he heard only whispers, rustles, babbles. Then one voice rose clearly above the rest. "Countless are the stories," it said. Then sleep took him, and he knew no more.

QUESTIONS

♦ ♦ ♦

CROW awoke early. With his bow in his hand, his quiver on his back, and a pouch of dried corn at his side, he set out again. The sky was blue, bright and clear, the air sweet with the clean scent of the nearby pines. Soon the lodge was far behind, and he was walking again among the towering maples and oaks of the forest. The sun was warm, but the air was cool. Green leaves still fluttered on many trees, but there was a dry, powdery smell of crisping vines and curling leaves, and the glint of red and gold shone everywhere.

Easily he shot birds, offering prayers of gratitude to the spirit of each. It was something he felt that he must do now that he knew the tale of Sky Woman and Creation. *They are my relations,* he thought. Then he sighed. *But how Grandmother would be pleased,* he thought, *if only she could see me shoot like this.* He sighed again. Then he set off for the Stone's clearing.

"*Dadjoh!* Welcome!" called the Stone when Crow approached.

"Welcome, Grandson. I call you that because I am old, oh-so-much older than you. And because we are related — as are all things. As you now know."

Crow laid down his bow, arrows, and knife among the ferns and climbed up on the Stone, setting the string of birds down beside him. The great round Stone was pocked by centuries of rain. Tiny holes and pits, like pores on skin, dotted its surface. And it was warm. Resting in the morning sun, the Stone radiated the warmth of a living thing. The hard, pinkish granite shone and glittered with flecks of mica that mirrored the sun. Thick veins of white quartz threaded the Stone's surface too, disappearing under the soft coat of green moss. Stone it was, but it lived too.

"You asked yesterday," began the Stone in its deep, calm voice, "how ducks and geese, pike and muskrat could have been in the waters before Good-Minded created them."

"I did, Grandfather. It puzzles me. You say we are related. And I sense that it is true. But how is it? You are part of Turtle's shell from before the time of Good-Minded."

The Stone chuckled. Then, "Good, good," it said. "You think well. But you must have patience. Long long ago, in the world before this one, it was like this. There were many kinds of Sky People. Many shapes could be taken. When Sky Woman was falling, certain Sky People saw her danger and need. At once they became the ducks and geese, pike and muskrat that were needed. Turtle rising from the waters was like that too. In those long-ago days when the earth was new, things like that, mysterious things, could happen. We are all related, Grandson, from that Long-Ago Time."

"Hmmm," said Crow, nodding his head sagely like the old men did in Council. "But, Grandfather, what happened to Good-Minded and Hard-Minded?"

"Ah, Grandson, it was like this. Hard-Minded wanted to gain power over Good-Minded. Such a thing could never be, but always Hard-Minded wished for it. He asked Good-Minded many times to tell him what might injure him, to reveal what his weakness might be. But Good-Minded saw the desire for power tangled in those words and pitied his brother, pitied the weakness he so clearly saw there. So sometimes he said, 'Oh, the leaves of the cattails will destroy me,' or sometimes, 'deer horns.' And each time, Hard-Minded went and got those things and attacked Good-Minded. But always to no effect. It was sad for Good-Minded, who realized that, while Hard-Minded could never destroy him, he still must subdue Hard-Minded for the sake of the earth and all the many living things, lest they be harmed. Then they battled in earnest. They battled for a long time. At last, Hard-Minded was driven deep underground and confined in a dark cave. But even there he woke dark creatures, powerful and hard-minded like himself, to dwell with him in the underground world. Always he tries to release them to do mischief on this earth. But Good-Minded left many determined helpers to keep them in check. Then Good-Minded himself took the Sky Road and returned to the Above World."

"Grandfather," the boy now asked, "at death, do all people follow the . . . the Sky Road?"

"Not all, Grandson," answered the Boulder. "You have seen the great forked band of the Milky Way? It is the Soul-Path. The split shows that there are two trails. At death, each person must choose the one they would follow. What they have done in life will determine that choice. One path leads to the Above World. The other leads down to the realm of Hard-Minded."

The boy was silent. "My parents and sister . . . ," he began.

"I cannot answer," answered the Boulder. "I do not know all things, only some, only a small piece of the story of our world. But think of how they lived and of how they treated others. As to chance and destiny — for I remember your final question — even the least things have meaning. All are rooted in causes that began long ago. Even so, destinies may change in a moment. Sky Chief uprooted a tree to see beneath its roots. It seems foolish. Because of his whim he lost Sky Woman. Yet from it too came the creation of our world." The Stone paused. Then it said simply, "Compared to me even the most ancient trees seem to pass their lives at a run. Your span of days is to me no more than that of a tiny bug. And yet we are linked. And you, Crow, must know the stories. So I will tell you stories. They show what happens."

"I am listening, Grandfather," answered Crow.

"Now, let me see. How did this go? I have had no one to tell it to for a looooong time. Ah, like this, then: Long ago, people and animals could talk to one another. Animals might even take the shape of human beings if they wanted, and people could become animals, for the powers of wish and dream were very strong.

One day, in that Long-Ago Time, a boy wandered out from his village, hunting. He took a new trail and followed it. Farther and farther it led, and on and on he walked. In time, he stepped from the forest out onto the plains. It was like a new world to him, that sea of tall grasses and rolling hills, so different from the woodland world that he knew. Curious, he continued on. After a time he lost the trail and could not find the way to return. Only the sea of waving grasses and endlessly rolling hills extended in every direction all around him. Only the vast sky extended endlessly above. He searched and searched for the way back, but to no avail. In despair he threw himself on the ground and wept bitterly, clutching at the yellow grasses. For a long time he lay there yearning with his whole heart to return to his village, his family, and his people.

It was getting dark when he stood up again. The sun was setting, and twilight now spread across the vast horizon. Not far off he saw a group of people seated around a fire, deep in conversation. Hesitantly he approached, hoping to find companionship and guidance home. Still, as these were strangers, he did not show himself at once, but rather hid for a time in the long grasses listening to their talk. Imagine his surprise when he discovered they were talking about him!

Then an old woman rose to her feet, walked calmly over to

where the boy crouched hidden in the grasses, and in a kindly voice said, "Come. I have adopted you."

He stood up, wiped his eyes, and answered, "Please, won't you show me the way home?"

"Not yet," said the old woman. "For there are things you must learn first. But do not fear. In time you will safely go home."

Then she led him to her lodge, and he dwelled there with this kind, old woman.

Her people were strange to him. They never hunted but instead wandered together in large groups over the plains. The men's heads were dark and shaggy, and they wore dark shaggy leggings, too. He began to learn their songs and dances, their ceremonies and medicines. In time, he knew almost as much as the people he traveled with. Yet, somehow, it all seemed strange, like the wanderings in a dream. And though months went by and he had many good adventures and times of happiness and became wise in the ways of his new people, he yearned always to return home.

Often he went to his foster mother and said, "Please, will you now show me the trail home?"

She would smile a bit sadly and answer, "It is not time yet. You must learn more. Be patient. Soon you shall return."

One night the boy was awakened by the beat of a distant drum. The beat was slow and steady. Yet he could feel it reverberate through the earth. It made his heart beat slow, slow. The sound made his loneliness all the worse. He went to his foster mother and said, "Please. I must return home. I can stay no longer. I feel as if my heart will burst with longing."

She smiled and said, "Now the time is close for your return. Now I will tell you all. The drum is the signal of the great buffalo chief. He is a tyrant. When he drums, he wishes only to show off his strength. He has no care for the welfare of his people. No, instead he calls them to a great race. Many die in the rush to come to his lodge far in the West. Many of the young are lost or injured. And when all arrive he will choose one to race with him, and race that one must. Alas" — she sighed — "the buffalo chief always wins and the loser dies. It is horrible. Soon he will sing. Then we must all go."

"But why must you go?" asked the boy, confused.

"Because we are buffaloes," answered his old mother.

Then the boy saw at once that it was true. He had been living with the buffaloes all these months and, while there had been many signs and hints of it, he had never before clearly seen the truth!"

The Stone paused. He asked, "Grandson, do you know what a buffalo is? They live far away from these thick forests and rushing streams. Can you picture this animal with your mind?"

"It is larger and heavier than either the leaping stag or the great, splay-horned moose that wades among the water lilies and plows through the winter's snow, is it not, Grandfather?" answered Crow.

"Indeed," answered the Stone.

"Once, in one of the times when trading was still safe, a Huron trader came to our lodge," said the boy, remembering. "He told of a time when his trading had carried him far to the West. And he described a large, curly-haired, humped-back animal with short, hooked horns and a fierce, generous mind. Thousands of these, he said, wandered in vast herds over a grass-covered country that rolled endlessly on. Yet he had seen hunters there, skillful as wolves, frighten them. The buffalo ran over a cliff and died, and the people gratefully butchered them and carried home much meat and many hides. The man said the ground shook and the dust rose up so high, it hid the sky. He had been frightened, he admitted, but he laughed as he recalled and told of it. He said he had thought then that the world was ending, the earth was shaking so. He had never seen or felt anything like it. He said that hundreds of the huge animals tumbled down over the cliff and were killed. Yet countless more roamed on. Their numbers seemed endless. From that one hunt the people had enough dried meat for many moons. They had new skins for lodges and winter robes and sturdy moccasins. They had bone, which they sharpened and polished for spear tips and arrow-heads, and they had stomachs for water bags. Those beasts, buffaloes, as you call them, were the great benefactors of those people."

"Yes, those are the mighty ones, the buffalo," agreed the Stone. "The bulls are fierce protectors of their own people. However, the great bull in this story, strong as he is, failed in that respect. His mind was not good, but *otgont*, evil."

Crow said, "Someday I should like to travel the great earth too. I should like to see buffaloes."

"Perhaps someday, Grandson," said the Stone, "you will. Let us go on with the story for now."

Then the Stone continued. "Soon the buffalo chief's song began. Then all the buffaloes began to run. Young and old, weak and strong, they all rushed together. For ten days and nights they ran, the boy running by his old mother's side. On the tenth night they arrived at a great hill on the plains. Then all the tribe ceased their mad running and flung themselves, exhausted and panting, on the ground. When the old mother had regained her breath, she said, "We have arrived. But it is madness. Many of the old ones have been abandoned. Many infants too are lost on the plains. Many are injured and weakened. Oh, my son, may this be the last of all such mad races. May you save us all."

"Me?" exclaimed the boy, panting still from the terrible run.

"Yes," said the old mother. "You have been chosen to race the chief. Do not fear. You shall win! You have the skill, and I the knowledge, to save you. Tomorrow when you wake, I shall bring you a bow and arrow. The winner in tomorrow's race must shoot the loser. Now listen. The chief's heart is protected. His ribs have grown together to make one great plate of bone that no arrow can pierce. If you outrun him — and I know you will — insist that he raise his hands. Tell him you need to see that he holds no weapons.

On his palm there is a red spot, a lifeline that leads to his heart. Shoot there and you will triumph. We have taught you all we know. We want you to teach your people. You see how we suffer. Do not forget our trouble. Run hard tomorrow. You can win!"

In the morning, when the boy awoke, he found himself surrounded by a great herd of buffaloes. Then one shaggy old buffalo cow ambled slowly toward him, a bow and arrow twined in the thick fur of her neck. She walked close, and he removed the weapons from where they hung in her tangled hair. He let his hand linger there, gently brushing the hairs of her mane.

As he leaned close, the old buffalo mother whispered, "Run well, my son. Our prayers go with you. The whole herd yearns for your success. The chief runs as a man, so remember, no matter what he says, shoot at the red spot on his hand."

Then a big, strong man with a dark, shaggy head of hair stood at the top of the hill and roared in a great bellowing voice, "A human boy is among us. I call him to a race."

Heart pounding, the boy walked up the hill to where the chief stood. "Boy," laughed the chief in his deep, strong voice, "you have no hope. I am an unbeaten, mighty champion. I am a great chief. And you, you are only a two-legged child. Why not give up now?"

"Let us run first," answered the boy quietly. "Then perhaps what you say will be clear to all."

"Ha!" snorted the chief fiercely, and he kicked the ground, sending up a puff of dry prairie dust.

All the buffaloes lined up in two great circles around the hill. The boy and the buffalo chief stood together. Then, with a great shout, the race was on.

Down the hill they ran, between the two circles of buffaloes. The boy could feel the hard-stamped ground pounding beneath his moccasins. His breath rushed, his heart beat, his lungs drew the air. The prayers and wishes of all the mighty buffalo people, mighty yet suffering, carried him, lifted him, so that his feet ran on and on and he did not tire. Still, the great chief ran mightily, too. Side by side they ran on. The chief grunted, "Run hard, boy. It is early yet. By twilight I will trample you into the dust."

The boy said nothing. He just ran.

Half the day flew by. The sun was high. The chief thought to rest. But no sooner had he flung himself down than the boy sped by. Up sprang the chief, and on they ran again. So it was, each time the chief thought to stop and catch his breath, the boy sprang forward, unyielding.

Toward sunset the chief flung himself, panting, down upon the ground and cried out, "Oh, I am beaten, disgraced. Shoot me and have done!"

But the boy knew the trick. "Stand and raise your hands," he said. "That way I will know you hold no hidden weapon."

Grinning, the cruel buffalo chief stood up and confidently raised his hands. How could the human boy know the secret of his power? He would humor the child, then attack! At once the boy let his arrow fly. But not at the chief's heart. No! He shot at the small red spot. The chief tumbled to the ground, his evil ways finished.

Then all the buffaloes shouted a great shout of joy, like thunder. They stamped the earth together and danced in a great rumbling circle around the boy, calling out in praise: "Deliverer! Brother! Friend!" For days they danced and feasted, honoring the boy who had brought them freedom. They gave him many gifts.

The new buffalo chief said, "We will never forget you. Whenever you or your people need our help, call upon us. The spirit of the buffalo is sturdy and tenacious. Our memory is long. We shall never let you down. Our help will always be given."

Then the great herds dispersed, each group going back to its own home. The boy returned with his foster mother to her lodge. There she taught him more songs, dances, and ceremonies. When she had taught him all she knew, she said, "I have taught you the wisdom of my people. The time has come for you to return. Share what you know with others. I am sorry to see you go. You have been a son to me in my old age."

She led the boy to the trail he sought. There the kindly old buffalo and the boy made their farewells. At last he set off for home. Following the trail, he came again to the forest and the ways he knew.

He came to his own village. But only a few very old people knew him. They had been the friends of his youth. But while they were now old, he was still young. Many years had gone by.

The boy rejoiced to be home. Yet he grieved too. His parents and grandparents were long gone. His friends were now elders, and many of them were already growing feeble. For a time he stayed alone, digesting the strangeness of his journey. Then at last he was ready to share all he knew. He taught his people everything. They sang the songs he taught them and they danced the ancient dances of the buffalo people. In time the boy became chief. The spirit of the buffalo kept the people of that village healthy and strong.

"Now it is done," said the Stone happily. "*Dah-neh-hoh*. I have spoken it. I have told the story of the Boy and the Buffaloes from the Long-Ago Time when this world was new. Do you see? Even a child, Crow, can change the destiny of a people. Was it mere chance that he came to the buffalo people? You decide. It is up to you. I shall rest now. But come back tomorrow. *A-ah-soh*. I will tell more."

"*Nyah-weh*. Thanks," answered Crow politely. "Yes, I will come, Grandfather. I will hear stories." He paused. Then he said, "But I want to tell Grandmother. She worries. I can see that I disappoint her. I want to tell her of your Long-Ago Time stories."

"Grandson," answered the Boulder, "you have a good heart. Perhaps your grandmother would listen and believe if you told her. But that is not the only reason you must not yet speak of this. Given enough time, even a tiny seedling becomes a sturdy tree. Good inner power — *orenda* — is like that. It must be nurtured until it is strong. Then, when you do speak, all will listen. It is not yet time."

"All right, Grandfather," agreed Crow reluctantly. "It shall be as you say — for now."

When Crow returned with a short string of birds, Grandmother said, "Is your power fading? If you hunt like this we will never regain our place among the People. Maybe you think we can just continue living here alone. But I am old and say to you that nothing lasts. Do not be lazy! The Hunter's Moon approaches. Then comes the Cold Moon. The Very Cold Moon stalks behind. Shoot birds!"

That night Crow lay tossing and turning miserably. The Stone offered wisdom, but it also placed tough burdens on him. Could it be trusted? *Otgont* creatures lurked, the creations of Hard-Minded. What is harder than stone? Perhaps the Boulder was setting a trap, leading him away from the new, happy life into destruction. Father had disappeared. Had he been killed by cold? Enemies? Or something else? Crow tossed and turned, unable to sleep.

NEW DAY

♦ ♦ ♦

WHEN the sun rose Crow rose too. The doubts that assailed him in the night had vanished like the passing of some evil dream. He stepped confidently from the lodge. "Grandmother," he said, "I am going out to hunt birds."

Grandmother nodded. She was busy sorting plants and herbs to dry for winter medicines. So Crow set off through the clearing and along the trail, hurrying deeper into the forest, shooting birds as he went and offering prayers.

"Ho! Grandfather!" he called when he at last entered the clearing in which the Stone rested.

"Ho! Grandson," answered the Stone. Crow approached and draped a string of birds over the Stone. Red, gold, and brown leaves spun down through the blue sky. Crow laid down his weapons and seated himself.

"Grandson," began the Stone, "You see how the leaves turn colors in the fall? Listen and I shall tell you how this first began. Long ago, in the world before this one, there were three young brothers. One day a hunter discovered the tracks of a giant bear circling their village. He rushed back to report his find. Soon all the people, including the three brothers, came to inspect the huge tracks.

No one had ever seen tracks so big. Even so, some of the warriors boldly announced that they would slay the monstrous bear. But the chief said, "Wait. Let us see what the bear intends. Perhaps it is a messenger and not an evil thing. And if it means us harm, the battle will be a fierce one and perhaps many will be injured or die. Let us wait and let us prepare."

Soon many animals began to disappear — deer, beaver, bear, panther, fox, and wolf. The great bear, it was decided, was eating them all. The meat racks of the village stood empty. There were few animals left for the people to hunt, and those that remained seemed unusually tense, alert, and wary, running off at the slightest whiff of even possible danger.

Then the chief said, "We have waited long enough, perhaps too long. But we have prepared a great store of weapons. We must kill the monster bear. It will be dangerous and difficult. But it must be done soon or we shall starve." Then a party of experienced warriors gathered and set out after the bear. For many days they tracked the path of the great beast. Torn trees, broken branches, ponds nearly dried and emptied of fish, piles of gnawed bones marked its way. At last they saw the bear standing on its hind legs, huge as a mountain against the sky, hungrily sniffing the air.

The warriors took arrows from their quivers, drew their bowstrings, and crept cautiously forward. When they were as close as they dared, they leaped to their feet and shot! The air filled with arrows. The bear roared so loudly that many men fell dazed and stunned by the terrible sound. Yet though many men fell, many bravely rose again to let their arrows fly once more. But the arrows seemed to have little effect. Not one could pierce the thick fur and hide of the monster bear. The bear dropped to all fours and charged, striking out with its great paws and biting with its sharp teeth. Soon all but two of the warriors lay dead or dying on the ground. The two who still lived ran back to warn their people.

There was much mourning and grieving in the village. Many had died. And still the meat racks stood empty as starvation stalked very close. At night the people could hear the coughing and chuffing of the great bear echoing from deep in the woods. Often too its huge tracks were found in the morning circling the village, as if it had contemplated tearing down the stockade and rushing in to devour the starving people as they huddled, exhausted, in their lodges.

Again a war party was assembled. Again the warriors tracked the monster bear and attacked. But once again the bear's charge was devastating. Many more men were killed, and still the bear roamed on unharmed.

The three brothers dreamed. They each dreamed that they tracked and killed the great bear. The dream came to each of them on four nights. Each night the dream was the same. The brothers talked together. "We must kill the bear," said the eldest, "and save our people. The dream gives us *orenda* — good inner power." The two younger boys agreed. Gathering their weapons, they set off alone on the trail of the bear.

They followed the bear's broad trail of destruction for a long time. At last, up ahead, they saw its mountainous form. Raising their bows, they ran toward the bear. Strangely, when the bear saw the three boys running toward it, their arrows ready to shoot, it turned and ran. It too felt the power of the dream. It too had dreamed the same dream as the boys. On each night, for four nights, it had seen itself die, killed by three boys. So the bear ran. Quickly the brothers followed. "See," shouted the youngest, "how it flees from us! The dream is true!"

The bear tore its way through the forest. Splintered branches and broken trees littered its path as it bolted on and on. And always the boys followed, never slackening their determined pace. At last the bear came to the end of the world. Mists rose from where the waters of the world poured off Great Turtle's shell into space. The brothers heard the roar of many waters falling. The bear stood poised and helpless there. Then it gathered its strength and, in one mighty leap, hurled itself into the heavens and ran on.

The boys too came to that final place where the world ends.

Mists rose and through that curtain of mist glimmered countless fiery stars. They looked at one another. Then, with only a moment's hesitation, they too leaped off the edge. On and on and on they ran, continuing the chase, never slackening their efforts, never halting or resting, racing ever onward among the stars whose fires now blazed above, below, and all around them.

That chase continues even today. The three young warriors still chase the great bear. On clear nights look up. You will see three stars follow a great square shape of stars like that of a bear. Through the seasons the mighty chase goes on. Toward the Moon of Falling Leaves, when the bear gets sleepy and slows, the hunters' arrows strike. Then red blood and yellow grease flow from the bear's wounds to stain the leaves red and yellow. So the leaves turn colors because of the great deed of those boys. Deeds make the world.

Though wounded, the bear escapes. For a time when winter lies heavy on the land, it disappears and sleeps. Then its wounds heal. Then too the boys rest at last. But, with spring, the bear awakes, and once more the eternal chase goes on. The three boys will always protect their people. They are vigilant and untiring. Because of them that monster bear has never returned to harm our good earth. *Neh-hoh.* Now it is done."

"A good story!" exclaimed Crow.

"It is," said the Stone. "And it is very old. And now you know it. But there is another tale about a giant bear and mighty deeds that you should also know. It was long ago, and it happened like this. You see, back then, long ago in the world before this one, two tribes were at war. Neither was victorious, and both suffered terribly. Good men died on both sides. Women and children grieved. Because of the constant fear of raids, many were reluctant to leave the safety of the village, even to gather food. Because so many skillful hunters were dead, there was less food for all, and so hunger was always close. At last, recognizing the foolishness of their ways, both tribes agreed to make peace. Orphaned children from one tribe would be adopted by parents of the other. Young men and women of each tribe would marry. In this way peace would be assured, not just for the present moment, but for a long time. It was a good plan.

The day came for the exchange of children and young people of marriageable age. Two groups set out journeying from one tribe to the other. But the eagerly expected visitors never arrived. And, strangely, no word came back from those who had left.

The people of one tribe grew suspicious. Perhaps it was a trap. Messengers were sent. But they too never returned. Then a swift runner was selected to travel to the other village and bring word back of what he saw. He left. Two days later a voice was heard crying from the trail. Runners went out. They found the messenger crawling back to the village, bloody from many wounds, his clothing torn.

"Niagwahe!" he gasped. "Monster Bear!"

They carried him back to the village. The chiefs gathered. "So it is not our former enemies," they said, "who harm us now, but Niagwahe. This is bad. Niagwahe is strong and has magic power. We need a brave man to hunt it down and destroy it."

The greatest old chief rose to his feet. "I hold aloft this sacred belt of white wampum," he said. "The man who takes it shall wear it always. He shall be known as the one who slew the Monster Bear and saved his people. Who will take it?" Not a warrior rose.

"Shame!" exclaimed the chief. "Is there no real man among us?"

The lodge was silent. The air grew heavy with tension. To lighten the moment and bring heart back to his warriors, the old chief turned to a boy who lived at the village edge with his grandmother. The boy was small, poor, and thin. He seemed slow-witted too, for he never said much but most often just watched and listened.

"Maybe you will take this and save us," joked the chief.

All the people burst into laughter.

At once the boy rose, took the wampum belt in his hands, and draped it over his shoulder.

The assembly grew quiet. The chief, astounded, asked, "Do you know what you have done?"

The boy nodded. Wearing the belt, he walked solemnly from the lodge and went to his grandmother. "I have taken the white wampum belt," he said. "I have agreed to save us from Niagwahe."

"Alas!" cried his grandmother. "You are a poor, foolish child. But now you must keep your word." She pounded parched corn and mixed it with maple sugar so he would have food for his journey.

The next morning the boy set out. As he walked he gripped the belt of honor and repeated a sacred pledge: "I will help my people. I will not yield; I will be yielded to. I will not run; my foe will run from me. I will not fail; I will succeed."

After two days he heard a loud thrashing from among the bushes ahead. A great roar filled the forest — the roar of Niagwahe, the Monster Bear!

Amazingly, the boy did not turn and flee. Instead, he cried out loudly in response, "I am coming after you! You cannot escape me!" and charged ahead.

The Monster Bear paused. Never had it heard such a challenge! What's more, the boy had flung at it the very words it always used to stun and dismay its victims: "I am coming after you! You cannot escape me!" The power of its own magic had been turned against it at last, and its spirit quailed. The great bear turned and ran! Behind it came the voice of the boy shouting, "Run! Run! I am coming after you! You cannot escape me!" Terrified, the Monster Bear, Niagwahe, ran on and on.

All through the day the chase went on. Now the sun began to set. Darkness settled over the forest. The boy knew he could go no farther. He had no hope of finding the bear in the night. He stopped to rest. He opened his pouch of parched corn and maple sugar. But

what was this! Maggots writhed in the pouch. The power of the bear had ruined his food. "No matter," said the boy. "I am not afraid of hunger. I will rest now. In the morning I will find the bear and destroy it."

The boy curled up beside the trail and fell asleep. He had a dream. In the dream the great bear crept humbly before him and meekly said, "I am defeated. But oh, let me live! At last I know the evil I have done in killing so many others. I lusted only for battle and victory. But I know now how precious life is. This fear has taught me and made me wise. I will never harm you or your people or their friends again. I will go far away to the icy north and hunt only the prey animals I need as food. I beg you, let me live!"

The boy awoke at daylight and smiled to think of his good dream. Then he set out on the trail.

In time he came upon the monster, Niagwahe. The giant bear sat rocking miserably on the ground, whimpering in defeat. The boy's unyielding spirit had triumphed over its own. "Do not kill me," it begged.

"Raise your foot," said the boy, aiming his bow. "I know your vulnerable spot is there."

"No, no!" cried the Monster Bear. "If you spare my life I will give you a gift of power, one to help you and your people forever."

"What is the gift?" asked the boy.

"My two great teeth," sobbed the bear. "I will shed them. They will give you power to protect your people. They are magic. He who holds them holds their magic power. And I will reveal a secret that will bring only good."

"Give me the teeth," said the boy, "and tell me your secret. I will spare you. But remember this day and the power of life and death I held over you."

The huge bear shed its two great sharp teeth. The boy shook them, and they became small enough to place in his pouch.

"My secret is this," said the bear. "Back along the trail is a cave. In it are the children and young men and women I captured. I have not devoured them yet. They still live!"

Then the gigantic bear rushed into the bushes and raced off toward the north.

The boy set off for the cave. A great rock blocked the way inside. From within the cave came pitiful wails: "Help! Someone, help!" The boy took hold of his white belt and announced, "I will not fail but will succeed!" Then, making a great effort, he set his shoulder to the stone and rolled it from the cave entrance.

Out from the darkness came the youths and children, blinking in the bright sunlight.

"Come," said the boy, "let us go home."

When he arrived leading that happy company, he showed the teeth of Niagwahe. He shook them, and they were large again. The people were astonished.

"How did you accomplish this?" asked the old chief in awe. "What magic power did you use?"

"I held tight to the white belt," answered the boy. "I was determined to help my people. I made up my mind to chase and not be chased. I vowed to succeed and not fail."

"Truly, that is a very great power," admitted the chief, nodding his head.

Then runners were sent to the other village, telling the whole tale. The two villages joined together at last. The orphans were adopted. The weddings took place. And so peace was at last restored.

"There. It is done," said the Stone. "I have told tales of the Long-Ago Time. Back then, huge creatures lived. Yet powerful as they were, even they could be overcome or made to change their hard minds. Now I will rest. Come again tomorrow and I will tell you more stories."

"I will, Grandfather," said Crow.

The sun's light was waning, and the shadows growing long. It was already late in the afternoon and that time of year when the days grew short. Crow gathered his weapons and headed for home. As he walked toward the village, the glow left by the stories faded to be replaced by a growing sense of uneasiness and guilt. Grandmother's lined, careworn face rose before him. He saw disappointment and anxiety written there. What would she think if she knew he simply sat all day, listening to stories, his bow cast idly aside? Still, even this thought could hardly rouse him to hunt earnestly. It was too easy for him now to imagine birds with stories of their own, stories that were silenced with each twang of his bowstring. For he now saw birds as living beings, fellow spirits, no longer simply as prey.

Grandmother was waiting anxiously. When he handed her the short string of birds, her shoulders slumped. She leaned heavily on her walking stick and sighed. "You have not brought many birds, Grandson."

"No, Grandmother," he said. He looked down. Her old, worn, deerskin moccasins stared back accusingly — "We have done our job," they seemed to say. "What of you?"

"I did not find many birds . . . before the light grew . . . too dim to hunt," Crow stammered. "The days grow short. Many birds have already left these woods . . . it seems. Those that remain are . . . hard to find."

Crow did not return to Grandfather Stone the next day. Or the next. In fact he stayed at the lodge, working and helping Grandmother for the next four days. He chipped arrowheads and gathered the last of the corn, squash, and sunflower seeds. He tied Grandmother's medicine plants into bundles and hung them to dry. He dragged wood back to the lodge and piled it inside the entrance. He gathered twigs and branches for kindling.

The leaves of the forest flared brightly and fell, carpeting the earth with the colors of flame. "Bear grease," smiled Gaqka as he worked.

"What was that?" asked Grandmother.

"Nothing," said Crow. But he longed to tell her the tale.

When the last of the herbs was bundled and hung, the last of the corn and seed gathered, the last arrow straightened, and the last twig stacked, Crow at last said, "I hunt tomorrow, Grandmother."

Grandmother nodded as she set a bundle of sassafras bark, good for making soothing tea, into a basket. Then she rose and, leaning on her cane, walked from the lodge. Her breath was labored. Her hip ached. She had to stop and rest as she walked. But she was not out gathering more herbs or roots for winter. She was heading for the village. The thought had been growing in her — something was amiss. Crow was not himself. He was hardworking and busy enough. But he did not hunt happily, and when he did, he returned with so few birds that it was as if some spell had been cast upon him. She would go into the village, though it made her angry and anxious to do it, and she would look for Crow's friend, Jo-ah-Gah, Raccoon. She had a plan.

She found Raccoon outside his lodge, hurling stones against a stump. *Thunk! Ka-thunk!* The women stacking wood and pounding dried corn into meal nearby looked suspiciously at Grandmother as she hobbled past them toward Raccoon. His round face looked up at her uneasily. He paused, his arm drawn back, then he turned and let the stone fly. *Thunk!*

"Grandson," said the old woman, seating herself on a log and leaning on her cane, "I have come to speak with you."

"With me?" exclaimed Raccoon, blinking in surprise.

"Yes. It is about my grandson that I would speak. Gaqka has a hunter's skill. Through the moons of spring and summer he went out and always returned with many birds. But now he brings hardly any. Some *otgont* creature may have cast its spell on him. He goes early, returns late, and . . . and I have come seeking your aid. If you will trail him and discover what lurks on the path he travels and tell me of it, I will reward you. Even if you find nothing, I will reward you."

Raccoon shook his head. "Grandmother," he said, "you are poor. What reward could you offer? Nooooo. I do not think so."

Grandmother's face tightened, and she rose, shamed and angry.

"But I will do it," continued Raccoon hurriedly, "for the adventure of it. It will test and hone my skills. Gaqka was always a fast runner. Though I was bigger, he always could outrun me. And if some evil creature lurks, I will fill it with arrows or lead the warriors to it. I will become a warrior and win honor and respect."

Grandmother nodded and rose. "It is good. I am grateful. Trail him tomorrow. He leaves at dawn." She hobbled from the village and started back along the trail, the *thump*, *thump*, *thumping* of the corn pounders fading slowly behind her.

TWO BOYS

◆ ◆ ◆

CROW trotted along the trail, dead leaves rattling and crumbling beneath his moccasins. The sun shone down through bare branches as he trotted on amidst a golden rain of falling leaves.

Raccoon followed, skirting the trail, keeping Crow just in sight. *Whatever it is, I will face it. I will be a warrior,* he thought. Yet his heart beat too with dread, for he was already far from the village, out where enemy warriors might lurk behind any tree.

Crow raced along, feeling little need for stealth. He did not raise his bow or slow his pace to seek birds. For now, he already had his offerings ready to present to Grandfather Stone. He would hunt later and bring fresh game to Grandmother — if he could tear himself away from Grandfather Stone and his stories in time. He wanted Grandmother to be proud of him again, and to be happy. But he wanted to hear stories of the Long-Ago Time too. He had tried to stay away and to focus only on what Grandmother might need or want him to do. But now that he had reentered the forest, the stories drew him. So he ran swiftly on. The sun shone. Leaves fell. Clouds coiled and uncoiled in ever-shifting shapes overhead. Soon the clearing was in sight.

"Ho! Grandfather," announced Crow, raising his arm in greeting. "I have come."

"*Dadjoh!* Welcome, Grandson," came the familiar reply. "I have been waiting. Days have gone by."

Raccoon, hidden behind the trees at the edge of the clearing, nearly screamed. His eyes opened wide, in shock. His heart beat rapidly. The hard edges of the known world wavered, and he seemed to slip across a line into another world, older and stranger by far than the one he knew. For a strong, deep, old, patient Voice had answered his friend Crow. And the Voice had seemed — he was sure of it — to rise from the boulder. Raccoon watched and listened with great growing uneasiness.

"Yes," said Crow. "There were things I had to do to help prepare for winter. They are done. Now I bring gifts, for I have come to hear stories." He slung his quiver from his back and slid out two arrows, placing them on the Stone. He put three flint arrowheads beside them, and from a small deerskin pouch, he poured out a handful of sunflower seeds and dried corn. Lastly he set down several shell beads.

"Your good gifts deserve gifts in return," said the Stone. "Sit, Grandson. I will tell stories."

When Crow had climbed up and settled himself comfortably, the Stone began. "Grandson," it said somberly, "the story I would tell today may scare you."

Crow thought for a moment, then asked, "Does it end happily, Grandfather?"

"Yes," answered the Stone. "The ending is happy."

"Then tell it," insisted the boy.

So the Stone began. "A boy and his grandmother were living far from the village. The boy's name was Osoon, or Turkey. They were poor. The lodge was big enough for many people, but they lived alone, for all the others of their family had disappeared.

Winter was coming, and the task of gathering enough firewood and food to last the winter was a hard one. The old woman wept every day for loneliness and for the difficulties before them. One day her grandson, Turkey, asked, "Grandmother, why do you weep so? We have each other. Soon we will have enough firewood, and we can live on roots and bark and dried corn till spring."

"Ah, Grandson," answered the grandmother. "What you say is true. But I have memories of another time. I remember good food and warm fires. And I remember other things too. Come."

She led Turkey to the back of the large lodge. She pushed aside a piece of bark. There was another room there, and it was filled with bark and horn and shell rattles; with drums, lacrosse sticks and balls; with fine clothing, bark boxes, and baskets; with carved bone combs, clay pipes, bows, arrows, clubs, fish spears, and digging tools. It was like a treasure house!"

Crow drew in his breath sharply. The Stone's words were triggering painful memories of his own past life and of his own lost home.

"These were used by our family," said Grandmother. "All the people — mothers, fathers, brothers, sisters, aunts and uncles; nieces, nephews, cousins, all, all are gone. This is why I weep. I weep for the hardness of the present and for the joys of the past now gone."

The next day, when Grandmother went out gathering wood, Turkey pushed aside the slab of bark and entered the room of treasures. The light was dim, but gradually he could see well enough. He found a large drum and sat there, surrounded by the treasures of his family, tapping the drum. It made a warm, resonant sound, like the beating of a heart. He remembered things: voices of a family, of many people talking; smells of good food cooking; the touch of soft hands; the warmth of laughter.

After a time he rose, left the room, and drew the bark cover back in place.

When Grandmother returned, he asked, "Where has our family gone?"

Grandmother answered, "Our family has all been destroyed by an evil sorcerer! His lodge is to the east beside a patch of giant strawberries, large as hearts. Once a village of our people lived there, but the wizard, drawn by the good berries, came and drove the people away, killing many. Now the village has rotted into the soil, and he guards the berry patch fiercely, killing all who come and eating their flesh! Oh, he is a monster! Do not go near him, Grandson! Travel north, south, and west, but never, never to the east!"

The next day Turkey went into the treasure room again. This time he took out a lacrosse stick and ball. He played. It felt good to run and toss and catch the ball, to fling it with a *whoosh* and a rush wherever he chose. Then he took out the drum and began to beat upon it. *Boom! Boom! Boom!* He beat it loud and hard. Grandmother came running. "Stop, Osoon! Stop, Turkey! The wizard will hear and come and eat us up!"

"Tell me of the wizard, Grandmother," said Turkey.

"His name is Deadoendjadse, and he lives with his seven sisters. All of them are cruel and hard-hearted. They have hearts stony as flint, hearts you would cut your hands on to hold."

"Make me moccasins," said Turkey.

"I will," said Grandmother, "but you must not go east in them. Promise you will not go east."

The Stone paused. "Someone is listening nearby," it said suddenly.

"I see and hear no one," said Crow, looking around in surprise.

"Grandson, you were attending well to the story," said the Stone. "But I was telling it. There is someone else listening. Tell the one in hiding to come forward and join us."

So Crow stood up and cupped his hands before his mouth, calling, "Come! Show yourself! Come! You too may sit here and listen!" Still, he saw no one.

Then a shadowed figure rose hesitantly from among the bushes. The next instant it turned and began racing madly from the clearing, back toward the village.

"No! Wait!" cried Crow. "Stop! Do not go! Do not tell!" Crow leaped down from the Stone and began running after the form disappearing rapidly into the forest.

It was a boy, larger than he and stockier. He ran well, but Crow, though smaller, was lighter and faster. So, despite his head start, soon the back of the panting figure approached. A quiver bounced on his back; a bow was in his hand. The boy leaped logs and bushes and ran on furiously, never looking back. Crow made a mighty effort and leaped desperately forward, hitting the runner just below the shoulders with his outstretched hands. The two boys tumbled to the ground and rolled to a stop.

"Jo-ah-Gah! Raccoon!" exclaimed Crow, sitting up, rubbing his shoulder, which he had bruised in the fall.

His old friend looked at him, anxious and puzzled. He was rubbing his knee. "Gaqka. Crow. I . . . I didn't know what was chasing me. I . . . feared. There was talk of a sorcerer. Who was talking? I heard a Voice. Not your voice, but one that was old and strong. It gave me the chills. Can a stone speak? Oh, tell me what is happening. Is it danger?"

"Grandfather tells the story of Turkey and his grandmother," answered Crow. "Come. Come back with me and listen. You are welcomed. Grandfather knows tales of the Long-Ago Time. There is no danger except that of knowing more than you know now, of knowing of the Long-Ago Time. It may change you. But for the good. Come with me. We will listen together. Grandfather Stone invites you."

"Grandfather Stone?" repeated Raccoon, puzzled. "Who is that?"

"Come," laughed Crow. "You will see."

Slowly Raccoon rose and began to walk back toward the clearing with Crow, who laughed merrily at his old friend's reluctance. Crow was happy that he would have a companion in hearing the tales, someone he could talk with about all that was happening. And Raccoon was someone he could trust. He felt better than he had for many days.

When they reached the clearing, Raccoon came forward suspiciously, gripping his bow, an arrow set to the string.

Crow said, "There is no danger. Lay down your weapons. We will hear stories."

But Raccoon held tight to the bow and arrow, though he bravely followed Crow forward.

Then the Stone spoke, saying, "*Dadjoh!* Welcome."

Raccoon's eyes flew open wide, and he nearly jumped straight up into the air. Though he didn't, his arrow did, flying up and arching across the clearing to disappear with a rattling sound among the branches of the trees. It was the Voice he had heard — the old Voice. And it was, indeed, coming from the Stone — as he had feared.

Crow tapped Raccoon on the shoulder and nodded. "We come, Grandfather," he said. "This is my friend, Raccoon. He will listen."

The Stone said, "He has already listened well. He can hear stories of the Long-Ago Time. He is ready. Sit."

Crow climbed on the Boulder and sat comfortably. Raccoon paused. He stood fidgeting uncomfortably. Then he took a breath, nodded his head and, dry-mouthed, answered softly, "I will listen."

The Stone answered, "It is good. You have courage. Put down your weapons and seat yourself beside Gaqka. Place a gift down beside you. For now, anything small will do."

Raccoon stood there, but his legs didn't seem to work. At last, he took a small step forward. Then he took another, gingerly approaching the talking Stone, closer and closer. At last he set down his weapons and, keeping his eyes on the Boulder, took a deep breath, climbed up, and seated himself beside Crow. He untied a small speckled hawk's feather from his vest and set it on the Stone, weighting it with a pebble.

"Now you too will hear Long-Ago Time stories," began the Stone calmly. "Do you remember the story?"

Raccoon nodded his head slowly. "I . . . I think so. Yes."

"Good," continued the Stone. "For it was like this — Turkey, you recall, asked for moccasins, and Grandmother said, 'I will make you moccasins, but you must not go east in them. Promise me you will not go east.' But Turkey, I now tell you, said nothing.

Grandmother made the moccasins. Turkey put them on. He went to the storeroom and took a bow and a quiver of arrows. Then he left, heading east. In time, he came to a clearing. He crept quietly through the bushes and peered at the clearing. Strawberries were growing there, large and red as hearts! In the center of the clearing was a long pole, and fastened to it by a bark cord was a human skin turning and twisting and swinging in the wind. Turkey crouched down. *So*, he thought, *the wizard has a watchman. I will have to find some way to approach unseen or Skin Man will surely alert his master.*

A little mole was creeping quietly among the grasses. Turkey bent low and humbly said to her, "Grandmother, help me. I am poor and need your aid."

The mole lifted up its head, squinted its tiny eyes, and in a little, high squeaky voice answered, "What is it you need, Grandson?"

"Grandmother, lend me your skin. I am here to end the ways of the evil sorcerer but I must speak with Hadjoqda — the Dried Skin — to make my plan."

"Yes, you may borrow my skin, Grandson," said the little mole. Then magically Turkey entered the skin of Mole and, burrowing under the ground, made his way quickly to the center of the strawberry patch. He broke a root into tiny beads and stained them with berry juice so they looked like real wampum beads. Then he rose up at the base of the pole.

Skin Man flapped in the breeze overhead. Then Turkey said, "Ho, brother! Let's talk. I have brought wampum in exchange for some good words. Will you talk with me?"

Skin Man looked down and saw a little mole. "Yes," it whispered in a voice soft as rustling leaves, "I will speak — for wampum."

"Then tell me of the clearing, brother," asked Turkey.

The Skin Man answered in a voice soft as rain, "This clearing and strawberry patch belong to the evil sorcerer, Deadoendjadse, and his seven sisters. They eat the sweet berries and never give me any, never any. The sisters grind human flesh in a mortar with white corn and feed my cruel master. It is they who guard the berry patch, keeping the deer and rabbits and raccoons and all the animals from the good fruit. They alone eat the berries. They alone," sighed the Skin Man softly as he swayed and turned in the breeze.

"What more should I learn to be safe?" asked Turkey. "For I would free the strawberries so all may eat."

"What will you give me?" whispered the Skin Man.

"I will rub my hands on you," answered Turkey, "and make you whole. You shall be free. And then I shall let you eat berries to your heart's content."

"I will tell you all you need to know. I will help you," said the Skin Man. "It is like this. The sorcerer and his sisters believe they are safe from harm. They think they are so safe, they can do whatever they want to anyone and that they can never be harmed in return. But no one knows what I know: They keep their hearts under the wing of a loon that swims in a tub of water beneath a bed in their lodge. Yet what can a poor Skin Man do? Yes, what can I do? For a fierce dog sits beside the bed and guards the loon that guards the hearts. That is the secret of their evil power."

Just then women's voices could be heard calling, "Hadjoqda! Dried Skin! Come to us!"

"Is the sorcerer with his sisters now?" asked Turkey.

"No, he is gone," said Skin Man.

"It is good," said Turkey with a smile, "that you have told me all this. For now we shall have them. Here is my plan: Go to the sisters. Give them the wampum. Tell them you have made it for them. I will drive the deer into the strawberry patch. The sisters will rush out to chase them away. Then I will enter the lodge, find the hearts, and destroy them all!"

The Skin Man smiled as he turned in the breeze. "It is good," he said. "Yes, today, at last, is a good day."

Then Turkey burrowed down into the earth and returned to Mole and gave her her skin back. "Thank you, Grandmother," he said to the little mole. "Soon, in exchange for your kind gift, I shall bring you strawberries big as hearts for you to eat."

Skin Man got down from his pole. Wavering and bending, he walked slowly toward the lodge, where the sisters called. "I have brought wampum," he said. "Gifts for my seven lovely mistresses."

The seven sisters took the wampum and were pleased. "Is all well with our delicious strawberries?" they asked.

Skin Man answered, "Very well."

Then Skin Man returned to guard the berry patch. Soon, many deer bounded into the patch and began to feed.

"Help! Help!" called the Skin Man in a voice like the rasping of sticks and leaves in the wind. "Deer are eating the berries!"

The seven sisters rushed from the lodge to drive the deer away. As soon as they were gone, Turkey stepped into the lodge. A bony dog lay beside a bed, guarding it. As he entered, the dog rose to its feet and began to growl. *Grrr. Grrr. Grrr.* But Turkey threw it a piece of meat and the dog lay down, wagging its tail contentedly, and began to eat. Then Turkey lifted the bed. There swam a loon in a pool of water. Round and round swam the loon. "Raise your wing!" ordered Turkey, raising his bow. The loon raised a wing. There were no hearts. "Raise your other wing!" ordered Turkey. There were eight tiny hearts.

Turkey grabbed them. They were cold and hard and sharp. But each pulsed with life.

Turkey ran outside yelling, "I am Turkey and I have your hearts. I am Turkey and I have your hearts!"

The sisters heard and, with a shout of rage, ran back to the lodge. They approached, raising sticks in their hands. But as they got close, Turkey squeezed the hearts, and they fell down in a swoon. He released his pressure, and they rose to attack. Once more he squeezed the hearts. Once more the sisters fell.

"Ho ho!" laughed Turkey. "I can make you dance!" Running before them, he squeezed and released the hearts. The seven cruel sisters, chasing him, fell and rose over and over.

"Enough!" cried Turkey. "You have killed many people and hurt many families. Now it ends!" He led the sisters on until he came to a flat stone stained with blood and surrounded by bones. It was here that the evil sorcerer and his sisters killed their prey. He threw seven of the hearts against the stone. The hearts shattered like flint. The seven sisters fell and rose no more. It was done.

But it was not yet over. The cruel sorcerer, Deadoendjadse, had heard the tumult and now came striding fiercely out of the woods. He came to the Skin Man, who dangled on his pole above him. Skin Man laughed exultantly in a voice like smoke, "Turkey has killed your sisters! Turkey has won!"

"Never!" roared the sorcerer and, raising his great club, he struck Skin Man from his pole, crushing him to the earth, then ran toward the lodge.

Skin Man lay folded in the dirt. "Turkey has won," he whispered again, "has won."

Roaring with rage, the sorcerer rushed at Turkey. "I will kill kill kill you!" he screamed.

"You will not!" said Turkey, who flung the last heart, the biggest of all, with all his strength against the stone. The heart broke with a great *crack*! and the evil sorcerer, Deadoendjadse, fell with a crash to the ground, never to rise again.

Turkey gave a yell of triumph and ran to the berry patch, calling, "Skin Man, we have won!"

But Skin Man was not on his pole. Turkey looked. There lay Skin Man, folded and beaten into the earth. Quickly Turkey bent down.

"I am glad you have triumphed," whispered Skin Man with a groan. "Now it is done."

"Not yet," said Turkey. "For I said you would live and eat sweet berries to your heart's content." Then he rubbed his hands gently over Skin Man, patting and massaging life back into the empty skin. And what was this? Skin Man's body began to fill out. He sat up. He was whole and well! He was a person, not a Skin Man now.

"Ah, I am glad to see you whole and well," exclaimed Turkey joyously. "You have been my companion into danger and together we have triumphed over great evil. I am grateful. My name is Turkey. Let us be friends."

"If you are Turkey," said the young man, springing to his feet, "then we shall be more than friends. I am your own brother! You were just a baby when the evil sorcerer came and killed our family and took me as his servant. It was horrible. But you, little brother, you have freed me and brought me back to life! And oh, but it feels good to again walk freely on our Mother Earth!"

Then how the two brothers embraced and rejoiced together to

have triumphed over such danger and to have found each other so miraculously again.

But Turkey said, "Brother, it is not done yet. Let us restore our family." So the two brothers went to the pile of tangled bones.

"Help me, brother," called Turkey. Then Turkey and his brother pushed a tree that grew beside the stone. They pushed and pushed. At last, when the tree began to totter, Turkey yelled, "Rise, bones! The tree falls. Rise now or be crushed forever!"

With a great rattle and scramble the bones leaped together and became people, who raced to safety just as the tree fell with a great *crash*!

Many people stood there. Turkey's mother and father and aunts and uncles and cousins. Many others from other villages as well. All had been victims of the evil sorcerer, Deadoendjadse, and his cruel sisters. But all were now whole and well, though some were a bit lame and some looked somewhat different than they had in earlier life. You see, in the mad rush to reassemble themselves and escape, some of the bones had become mixed together, a leg from one joined to the body of another. Still, they were overjoyed to be alive.

"Now it is time," said Turkey. "Let us go home." Just then they heard a howling from the lodge. Turkey fingered his bow. Then he turned to his brother with a questioning look.

The brother said, "The dog was just a servant. It too was misused."

"Come, dog," called Turkey. The dog dashed eagerly from the lodge and raced to Turkey, leaping up and whining and licking him. Turkey and his brother and all the people laughed. Gathering his family at last, Turkey and the others set off together through the strawberry patch.

Turkey paused. "Grandmother Mole," he called. "Come and eat!" The little mole rose up from the ground. "I will, Grandson," she said. "Oh, I will."

When Turkey and his brother and his mother and father and his aunts and uncles and cousins came to the lodge, the old grand-mother wept aloud for joy to see them all, her own loved ones, again. She wept for sheer joy!

In time they decided to rebuild their village beside the berry patch, and so, taking their family treasures, they went there. Then they built new lodges and lived there with the others that Turkey had freed, making a new village.

And there they ate berries big as hearts to their hearts' content, sharing them with all. And there their descendants live to this day.

And now it is truly done."

"So that is a Long-Ago Time story!" exclaimed Raccoon. "Now I see why you've been coming and sitting here rather than hunting, Gaqka. I feel like such a sneak. Here are those two accomplishing so much together, and here I was just trying to spy on you, after all you've been through too."

"Well," said Crow, looking up at Raccoon seated beside him,

"I'm glad you're here. I haven't been able to tell anyone, not even Grandmother, about Grandfather Stone and the stories. Grandfather's been saying that I shouldn't tell anyone. Yet I know Grandmother has been worried, so that has been hard. But sometimes, I guess, things work out in ways you could never predict. For now I have a companion on this trail. As for spying, it looks to me like you almost bit off more than you could chew. And I'll be happy to remind you of how you ran off scared — if you ever get uppity. So, I'd say we're even."

"Grandmother sent me," admitted Raccoon. "She couldn't believe what a poor hunter you had become. She thought there must be more to it. She was right. But I never dreamed of what I would find."

"Well, that's something, at least," answered Crow. "To know she believes I'm capable of more." He sighed. "How am I going to fix this? I can't hunt like I used to. It's not that I'm not good at it. I am. It's just that . . . oh, I just can't."

"Maybe you already gave the answer," said Raccoon thoughtfully. "Maybe things work out, even when you don't see how."

"Sometimes. Maybe," answered Crow dubiously.

"The day goes on," interrupted the Stone, "and waits for no one. Have you settled your minds? Are you ready to listen to more stories?"

The boys nodded.

"Good. So, then, it was like this," began the Stone. "A tale of two who were like brothers. Long ago there were two boys. They roamed the woods, shot bows and arrows, played lacrosse, and trailed each other to hone their tracking skills. But always something else, something else seemed to tug at their minds. What could it be? They did not know. But they found they no longer felt at ease in their village. And indeed, so much time did they spend on their own, the village seemed to pay little heed to them. One day they decided to travel.

They set out. They traveled for many days and camped at night. Soon their traveling food of parched corn and maple sugar was eaten. Now they had to dig for roots and hunt for themselves. It was hard. They came to swampy ground. One boy thought he could never cross. The muck pulled at his legs so that each step took all his strength. "I can go no farther!" he cried out in desperation at last.

"You can! You can!" insisted his friend. "Take one step. Then take another! We are almost through!"

So it went. When one faltered, the other took the lead. Encouraging each other, they crossed swamps, traversed mountains, forded rivers, went through forests. One alone could never have made that journey, but the strength of the two combined made it possible. Still, no matter how far they went, something seemed still to call to them, and so they traveled on. One day the boys stood beneath a huge hemlock tree, its branches so thick, they drooped to the ground. It was like a ladder on which one could climb to the top. One of the boys handed his bow and quiver to the other. "Let me go up and see what can be seen," he said.

He climbed up and up and up, higher and higher. When he reached the top he could see far over the vast land. But he also saw extending from the top of the tree, a trail rising up into the Blue, into the Cloud-Sky World! Hurriedly he climbed down and told his friend, "I have found a trail to the Sky World! Let us take it!"

Excited, both boys climbed. When they reached the top they stepped hesitantly onto the Sky Trail. It swayed for a moment then was solid and held their weight. For a while they stayed near the treetop, fearful of falling. Beneath the edges of the trail they could see the trees and ground of this world far below. At last they came to believe the trail would hold them, and, gathering their courage, they set off at a brisk pace.

All looked just as it had in the world they had left behind, except that the trees and flowers were taller, the light brighter, the colors sharper, the air sweeter, the animals larger. They stayed on the trail. In time, they came to a bark lodge with smoke rising from the smoke-hole.

The older boy said, "It is the custom to enter a house that stands beside a trail."

"Yes," agreed the younger. "Let us go in."

The eldest pushed aside the bark entrance and stepped inside, followed by the younger.

A vigorous-looking man with a bright, cheery face sat beside the fire. A great disc of mica hung on the wall behind him, reflecting the fire's light and making the lodge bright.

"Welcome! Welcome, Brothers!" he called to them in a strong clear voice. "At last you come. I have called you and have watched your travels with interest. Be seated. I cannot stay for long, but let us talk."

The boys looked at each other, then stepped forward and seated themselves by the fire. The man continued: "This is my resting place. Each day at noon I come here. I am the one that people on your world call 'the Brother Who Lives in the Blue.' I am the Sun. All day I journey, but at noon I sit here, high overhead, and rest before racing on again. Oh, oh. Already I must leave. Follow the trail, Brothers! Speak to the old woman who lives in the next house. She will tell you more."

With that, the man leaped to his feet, hung the great shining disc of mica around his neck, and with a broad smile on his ruddy face, rushed from the lodge and was gone!

Amazed, the boys rose, and they too left the lodge, continuing on the trail in the direction they had been walking. In time they came to another bark lodge. When they stood at its door, the eldest said, "Our Brother Sun said we should enter."

"By all means," agreed the younger. "Let us go in."

In they went. There sat an old woman with a wrinkled face, sewing skins together to make clothes and blankets. A basket of porcupine quills dyed many colors was beside her, and she lifted one now to begin a bright pattern. A gentle fire burned before her. Steam rose from the pot hung above the flames. A dog lay curled by her side. But much else remained in shadow. She looked up and said, "Welcome, Grandsons. Your Elder Brother, the Sun, sent you here. I am glad you have come. I will give you food and we can talk, for it is a long time, I think, since you have eaten."

She brought a wooden bowl for each and ladled out two halves of a boiled squash and gave each a small piece of fry bread. "Eat, Grandsons," she said.

The boys looked. Suddenly they realized how hungry they were. "Grandmother," said the eldest, "we are very hungry. One of us could eat what you give and still be empty-bellied."

"Oh, no," said the old woman. "This food will never be exhausted. Eat and eat. Eat all you want."

The boys ate. The dog watched with interest, its tongue lolling out, a smile on its face. The more the boys ate, the more food there seemed to be. When they were done, they were full. Half a small squash and a piece of fry bread had seemed like the hugest of feasts!

"Grandsons," said the old woman, "I am the one they call Grandmother Moon. Now listen. The trail ahead grows dangerous. Whatever happens, you must walk straight on! Do not stop for anything, no matter what! And do not be tempted to step from the trail. Enemies lurk ahead, I warn you. Do not stop until you come to the third house. It is a good distance from here. You will be safe there. Now you must go. I have work to do, and time is short."

The boys thanked Grandmother Moon. The dog stretched and yawned, showing its pink tongue and white teeth, then walked over to them, wagging its tail. They petted the dog. "Good dog!" they said. Then they left the lodge and set out on the trail once again.

They walked and walked. The plants began to call to them, saying, "Take some of my fruit. Taste these berries. Try this leaf." The deer and bears and turkeys called, "Shoot me and roast my flesh!" The boys felt terribly hungry, though they had eaten well at the lodge of Grandmother Moon. But they remembered her advice and, bellies rumbling, walked straight on. Not once did they step from the trail. They walked on for a long time. At last, up ahead, they saw the third lodge.

In they went. There sat a sturdy old man with a wrinkled face and long white hair. "Welcome, Nephews!" he called. "I see you have come safely along the trail from Grandmother Moon. You have answered the call of your brother, the Sun. Now you are going to a great assembly. To enter, you must be changed. Your bodies of earth must be transformed to enter the assembly of the Sky World."

Then the younger boy anxiously exclaimed, "I do not want to be changed! I do not know what this means!"

"Change me," said the eldest. "I want to know all that happens. I want to see where every trail leads."

"Come," said the old man. "Do not be afraid." He set a large section of bark on a slant. "Lie down on this."

The oldest boy stretched out on the slab of bark. Then the old man blew through the spread fingers of his hand at the boy's head. At once the flesh separated from the bones. Two piles, one of bones, one of flesh, fell to the ground.

The youngest jumped to his feet and cried out in horror, "Alas, I am alone! My friend is gone!"

"Do not be afraid," repeated the old man gently. "Watch and see." Then the boy watched as the old man carefully lifted each bone and joint and washed it and wiped it clean. Then he laid the bones back down together and blew again. At once the flesh leaped to the bones, and there lay the boy, taller and stronger-looking and handsomer than before.

The boy leaped to his feet, his eyes bright and clear. "I feel good, Grandfather," he exclaimed. "My eyes see far. I can see out the door of your lodge and far far away. Everything is clear to me. Inside the lodge I see every crack and fissure in the bark walls. I can see easily where before all was only shadow and darkness. And I feel strong. Look!" The boy lifted his bow and shot an arrow. Out it flew through the open doorway and on and on it sailed until it was lost at last like a tiny speck, gone from sight.

The younger boy hesitated. Then he said, "I will follow the trail of my friend." Slowly he lay down on the slab. The old man blew. Away fell the flesh and bones. All was cleansed, washed, and wiped clean. Then again the old man blew, and there, once more, lay the younger boy, but he too was now stronger and taller and more handsome than before.

He too leaped to his feet.

"Try your powers," said the old man to the boys as he led them outside. He pointed to where a large deer stood grazing far off, near the trees.

"Chase the deer," said the old man. At once they raced off. The deer bounded away. They ran lightly, caught up with the deer and continued on effortlessly by its side. When the deer began to tire they turned and ran back to the old man.

"Thank you, Grandfather," they said humbly when they returned. They themselves were awed by their newly acquired power.

The old man smiled. "You are ready," he said. "Continue on the trail. A guide will appear."

The two boys set out. Up a rise they went. Just before they reached the top they saw another distant hilltop before them, higher than the one they now climbed. On it, far off, they saw a man. Down the man went along the trail, disappearing into the valley before their hill. In a moment he stepped up to the top of the rise just as they reached the crest of their hill. The boys were amazed. The man must have traveled very fast indeed to have reached the crest in concert with them, for they had only been a few steps away.

"Ah," smiled the man. "Your Elder Brother called and you came. That is good. Now we shall journey to the assembly."

They set off at what seemed the same ordinary walking pace, but the air whistled around their ears, their hair blew back, and their bodies felt chilled as if a great wind blew. They felt too as if things even they could not quite see, even with their new eyes, were streaming past at a furious pace. After a time they heard many voices talking. The voices were like music. The guide paused and said, "You have come to where you were summoned."

Before them spread a huge village. Many lodges were gathered by the bend of a shining river. "Walk among the people," said the guide. "Go freely anywhere you please. But do not enter the lodges. Even if you see a dear relative, a brother or sister who has left the earth and whom you may yearn to see, do not go into that lodge. Only those who have left the earth through the portal of death may enter there. But you may enter the great lodge of Haweniyo, the Creator. I will call you to enter when the time comes."

The two boys wandered through the village. Large fragrant flowers grew everywhere. Pools of clear water reflected the stars. At the same time, a bright yellow sun shone in a blue sky and a silver moon glowed overhead. It was strange, yet very beautiful. The boys heard laughter that faded into music so joyous, they lingered, standing silent and still, to catch each faint, fading note.

The guide stood before them again. "Come," he said. "The assembly begins."

The villagers were walking in throngs toward a beautiful lodge. The boys and the guide joined them. Clusters and knots of people became streams. Streams of people flowed into a great river of people, all of whom entered the great house. Inside, the walls were covered with green boughs that gave off the fresh odor of pine. Entwined among the boughs were flowers whose perfume was more wonderful than any the boys had ever smelled before. Its sweetness reminded them of the sweetest moments of their own lives. But they had no name for that aroma. Nor could they name the flower from which it sprang.

Soon dances of thanks and gratitude began. All the people danced, and the boys danced too. On the dances went, yet hardly a moment seemed to pass.

At last the guide said, "You were called to witness these things and to join the dance. Now you must return to Earth and tell your people of all you have seen. If people knew, then perhaps they might live well, respect the many living things, and be able to take the Sky Trail when the earth-life is past. For lack of this knowledge, many suffer. Now it is time to return. Come."

The two boys and their guide set off back along the winding trail. The wind again whistled in their ears and blew their hair back as they walked on. Things half seen streamed furiously past. When they came again to the rise, they paused. "Farewell," said the guide. "One day we shall meet again." Then he turned and in one, two, three paces was gone!

The boys came again to the lodge of the old white-haired man, and then to that of Grandmother Moon. At each they stopped and said farewell. They came finally to the lodge of their Elder Brother, the Sun, who welcomed them. "Ten days have gone by since you first arrived," he told them.

The boys looked at each other in surprise. "It seemed like only a day has passed," they exclaimed.

"Oh, it has been ten," said the Sun. "And I tell you, a day here is like a year on Earth. You will be grown men when you reach your people. But the village has been moved. Things are not as they were. Do not worry. You will find your people. All will be well. I will watch for you as I travel across the heavens each day."

Brother Sun traveled with them along the Sky Trail to the top of the hemlock tree that now extended a good height above the trail. The tree had grown. Time had, indeed, passed. "Farewell, Younger Brothers," said Sun.

"We are grateful, Elder Brother," said the boys. Then they left the Sky Trail and climbed back down the tree.

They traveled quickly to the village. But it was as Brother Sun had said. When they arrived, only grass-covered mounds of decayed bark showed where the lodges had stood. Tall grasses grew wildly in once carefully tended fields. The boys' eyes took it all in at a glance. Yet those eyes were now very keen. They saw the faint imprint of footsteps left on the earth from years before. Swiftly they ran following them. In time, they came to a new village.

The people hailed them, wondering, for the two were tall and straight and very beautiful. Light spilled from them. The people shaded their eyes and looked and wondered. "Young men," they called. "Who are you? Where do you come from?"

"We are boys of this village. We left years ago. The village moved, but we have found you. Does no one remember us?"

A middle-aged woman stepped hesitantly forward. "You look, I now think, like my little brother," she said to the oldest of the two. "But he has been gone ten years."

An old man stepped forward. "You seem to me now to look like my young son who disappeared ten years ago," he said to the younger. "People feared some evil creature captured you boys. So the village was moved to protect other children."

"Sister!" they exclaimed. "Father! It is us. We are home." And they all embraced, the two old people overcome for a time with emotion.

Then the boys announced to all the people, "We are they, the ones who were gone but are now returned. Gather tonight and listen, for we will tell our story. We have visited the lodge of our brother the Sun and our Grandmother Moon. We have danced in the lodge of the Creator! Where we have been there is only joy."

That night, when the people had all gathered, the eldest told the whole tale, concluding, "Ten days it seemed to us once we got there. Something called, and we went. But no more than ten days, it seemed," he repeated, looking around with shining eyes.

"This is our counsel," said the younger. "Know that a good trail leads to the lodge of the Creator. Those who treat others kindly, who live well, will go there and dance in joy. These things are true. Remember them."

The one who told the tale was named Speaker by the people. And the one who gave counsel was called Explainer. They lived there from that time on and had many adventures helping their people before they became old men.

"That is a tale of the two great travelers, Speaker and Explainer," said the Stone. "Alone, neither of them could have accomplished the journey. But together they were able to do it.

"Now it is time to rest. The shadows grow long. The days are short, and swiftly Brother Sun travels into the shadowed West. Come again. Come tomorrow and I will tell more."

The boys thanked Grandfather Stone, slid down, gathered their weapons, and headed for home.

Suddenly Crow clapped his hand to his forehead and exclaimed, "I forgot! I have to hunt birds for Grandmother!"

"I will help," said Raccoon.

The boys set off. When they had a short string of birds, darkness was already falling, and Raccoon asked, "Would you tell one of the tales you've already heard from Grandfather Stone? I like the ones he told today. Tell me another, would you?"

Crow hesitated, wrinkling his brow for a moment. "Oh, I don't know," he began lamely. "I'm just . . . all I've done is listen. I have never told anything to anyone before."

"You can do it," said Raccoon encouragingly. "I know you can. And how bad could it be? At least I'd hear something I've never heard before. Grandfather said I was ready to hear stories. Come on, Gaqka. You have been hearing Long-Ago Time stories. Now share one. It's only me listening, anyway."

"All right," said Crow. "I'll try." He paused and took a breath. "So, it was like this. Long, long ago, in the world before this one, there lived the chief of the Sky World and his young wife . . ." As Crow told the tale, they walked along the dark trails, going by feel now, led on by traces of starlight and by the light of a fitful moon appearing, disappearing, and reappearing from between high, thin clouds. Time and distance passed swiftly as the story carried them on. The trail, which had seemed long in the morning, now seemed short. Before they knew it, they had neared the village and the tale was done.

Raccoon whistled appreciatively. "I knew you could do it! You told it well. I could see the whole Sky World and the Creation. I won't forget that! You'll have to tell more stories sometime. That was good!"

Crow nodded. "Thanks. I may have forgotten some pieces, but it was mostly all there, I think. More or less. Anyway, thanks for getting me to try."

Raccoon nodded. Then he added abruptly, "I too forgot something! Wait here. I must speak with your grandmother before you enter the lodge. I trailed you because she feared some *otgont* creature had cast a spell. She expects her spy to slip ahead and tell her what was found."

"Okay. I'll wait. You trailed me well, you know," added Crow admiringly. "I never knew I was being followed."

"But you crackled the leaves," laughed Raccoon, "and loudly! It was not hard at all to follow your trail undetected. Even a little child could have done it!"

Crow, embarrassed, scratched his head. "It is true. I was careless. I was not thinking of hunting."

"Well, wait here," said Raccoon. "I will tell Grandmother I trailed you but that birds were hard to find. Very hard. Then I think I'm going to sit down somewhere and think about all that has happened today and all that I have heard, before I go on home."

Crow shifted his short string of birds from one shoulder to the other and cleared his throat self-consciously. "Wait," he said before Raccoon set off. "I . . . I want to ask you something."

"Ask," said Raccoon, turning back.

"Do you think," began Crow, "that I . . . that I did anything to cause Father's disappearance and Mother and Little Sister's death? Grandmother said some people think that."

Raccoon kicked a stone with his foot. It rolled into the underbrush, making a rattling sound. "That's foolish talk," he said. "You didn't do anything. Forget all that. I mean it. Do you hear? I am older and bigger than you, so when I say 'forget it,' listen to me.

Really. I heard my parents talk about it once, about what some people said, and they said it was all just stupid talk. Now, you tell me something — are you going back to Grandfather Stone tomorrow?"

"I am," answered Crow.

"I'd like to go too."

"Sure," said Crow. "We'll go together."

"At sunrise!" Raccoon laughed.

"Yes. And thanks," said Crow.

"For what?" answered Raccoon.

ALLIES

◆ ◆ ◆

Raccoon left Crow, walked a few hundred yards down the trail, and entered the old lodge. After a short time he reappeared framed in the doorway against the light flickering within. He turned to the woods, where Crow still waited unseen in the darkness, waved, and was gone.

Then Crow stepped from the forest's edge, walked down the trail, and entered. A fire was burning, and Grandmother sat beside it, stirring a kettle that hung over the flames.

"You must be hungry and cold, Grandson. Come sit here by the fire."

"I have brought birds, Grandmother. Look! More than last time."

"It is good," said Grandmother, taking the short string of birds he held to her. "Perhaps your power is returning. Was it difficult to find them?"

"It took a long time, Grandmother," answered Crow, looking into the steam rising from the soup. "I traveled far."

"Eat, Grandson," answered Grandmother. "I will be back." Grandmother lifted the door flap and was gone.

Crow ladled soup into a bark bowl. Outside, the wind whistled and branches creaked. He had been too tired and distracted to ask Grandmother why she was going out. Perhaps it was to at last speak with some old friend. More likely it was to gather medicine plants that must be plucked only when the moon showed the proper face or when certain stars appeared. If so, it might be disrespectful to the plants to even ask. They might become offended and the medicine would fail or even turn to poison. Besides, he was glad this night for some time alone.

When he was finished eating, Crow began plucking the birds. He removed the feathers, putting the stiff wing feathers suitable for fletching arrows into a bark box. The downy breast feathers he pushed into a deerskin pouch for Grandmother's use. Shirts, robes, and moccasins could be lined for winter with them.

What had these birds known in life? he wondered. Though small, they had a strong spirit. They stayed on each year, refusing to yield except in death to even the bitterest cold. Deep in winter, when the ground was frozen hard as stone, they might still be heard squabbling in the bushes. These small birds had power. So Crow's thoughts went as he plucked the birds and gutted them with his flint knife.

It was dark out along the trail, and Grandmother, feeling old and tired, moved slowly. *What was that boy up to?* she thought irritably. *Why was the hunting suddenly so hard? Had they done something wrong?* It made her angry to think like that, but now it was hard to avoid it. Raccoon had simply said the birds were scarce. But why was that? There were always causes, even if they were invisible. The darkness enveloped her, and the rustling of bushes, the creaking of branches, made her slow steps seem even slower. Her heart pounded. She wished she could be back at the lodge eating roasted birds and corn soup. If enemies lurked nearby she would be helpless and die where she stood, unable to run. But she would yell. Loud, she decided. Then they would not take Gaqka unawares. On she walked, pausing and resting, letting the pain of her hip ease off before she began again. But her mind found little ease from the nagging questions that plagued her.

When she came to the center of the village she hobbled to the longhouse of Donyonda — Eagle — Raccoon's father and, at one time, her son's good friend. She wondered if Raccoon would be with his father. She hoped not. She did not want the boy to know what she was preparing this time.

As she stepped closer, thoughts she had held at bay began to circle in her mind: *Eagle was a good man. But how will he act now that I am friendless and poor? His wife is no fool either. Blossoms Falling is a strong, smart woman. Still, will I be shamed by going to them? Well, I must go and see. Something is happening. I need allies, someone I can trust.* She paused before the longhouse. From it came the smoke of cooking fires and the smells of food and the voices of people talking. This was the life she and Crow too had so recently and happily lived — before all had been terribly changed. Old woman, she said to herself, why do you dawdle? The past is gone. Doorways are for walking through, not standing at.

She stiffened her back, took a breath, lifted the flap, and stepped into the smoky longhouse. Many people were there. A row of six fires burned along the center, below the open skylights. The great ridgepole of the roof, high above, was black with soot. Kettles of corn soup, savory with herbs and with deer meat, bubbled over the fires. Maize pudding and corn bread steamed on bark trays. She continued on, people looking at her in surprise, then turning swiftly away, as if she carried some bad sickness with her that they might catch. As if she were the sickness. She ignored the looks and murmurs, set her jaw, looked straight ahead, and hobbled on.

Eagle was seated on the sleeping platform near the center of the lodge. He was smoking, and his eyes opened wide when he saw Grandmother standing before him. *"Dadjoh!* Welcome!" he said stiffly. He lifted the pipe from his mouth, the pipe made of smooth, tan stone carved in the shape of a bird with hunched shoulders. He nodded, the crested band of hair along the central ridge of his head rising and falling before her like the edge of an eagle's wing. Blossoms Falling ceased scraping the kernels from a dried ear of corn with a deer's-jaw tool. She wiped her hands together. It was an

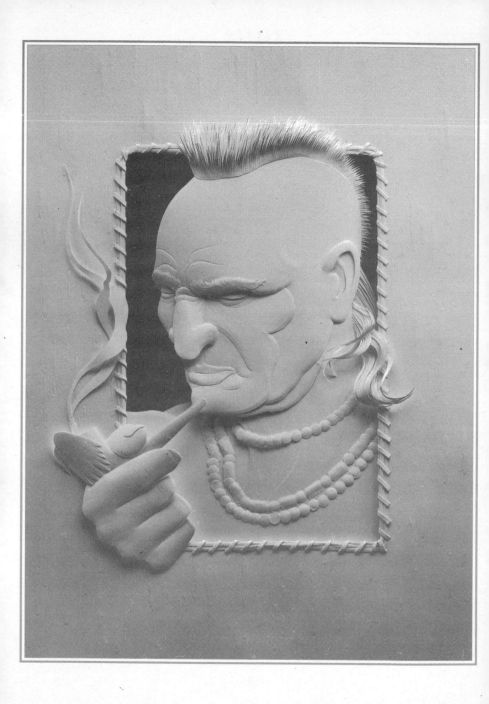

awkward moment. "I am letting the deer chew the corn first for me," she joked, her broad face cracking in a smile. It was an old joke. Grandmother smiled back, grateful for the courtesy, and nodded. "It is warm by the fire," said Blossoms Falling. "The night is cool. Come."

The others in the lodge looked away. It was not their business. Each fire had its own right to privacy. People cooked and ate and talked. They were polite. And they did not want to know of Grandmother's troubles. Why should they? Who these days did not have troubles? And if hers were heavy, surely she must deserve them.

Raccoon was nowhere in sight. Grandmother slowly seated herself. She held her hands out to the fire. "I know that these are hard times," said Grandmother at last. "So I have not come to beg. I do not expect help. Men must fight. Game is scarce. It is knowledge I need."

"What knowledge?" asked Eagle, intrigued.

"The ways of Gaqka. He has his father's hunting power. He fed us well with birds — at first. Yet now he returns with only a few birds."

She caught the swift glance that swept from wife to husband.

"Yes, I too know that he is young. And I know that many birds have left," she continued, "for Old Man Winter will soon be stalking our hills. And yes," she added, glancing up at the man and woman seated before her, "I know that I am old. And that old ones sometimes think strange thoughts. Still, it is odd. Gaqka is a fine bird-hunter." She weighed her next words carefully. "Jo-ah-Gah trailed him today, sunrise to sundown, and tells me only that birds are scarce. Yes, I asked him to trail Gaqka. But I think something is there, no matter what he reports to me. Perhaps . . . ," mused Grandmother, "perhaps I am old and foolish. But sometimes useless old women can see things that those busy with more important matters miss. Maybe some *otgont* power lurks. My son is gone, as is my daughter-in-law, and one grandchild. I will not lose Gaqka too. Will you follow him and uncover the truth?" she asked suddenly and fiercely.

The flames danced and hissed. Her long hair glistened like river foam. Her wrinkled face shone like cracked copper. Eagle and Blossoms Falling could see the many long, hard years etched starkly there. Many sorrows, many losses, and griefs.

Eagle puffed on his pipe and looked into the flames, looked and looked as if seeking to penetrate the shadows and grasp what was hidden and unknown. Smoke curled up from his bird-shaped pipe's back. He puffed and thought. He looked at Grandmother. He nodded. "Warriors will follow the boy with me. If there is danger, we will destroy it."

"Gratitude." The old woman sighed, rising wearily to her feet. "You have my gratitude. I ask nothing more."

Blossoms Falling asked, "You do not trust our son?"

"It is not that," said Grandmother slowly, careful lest she offend. "I think . . . I think there is something here that is more than any boy or any two boys can manage. I cannot say why I think this, but I do. Gaqka has been strange. He keeps some secret, and Jo-ah-Gah, I think, may — it is possible, they have been friends — may keep the secret too. He gives his trust to Crow and not to me. I should have thought of that when I asked for his aid. Now I have come to you. Now you know all. But I ask too that Jo-ah-Gah should not know of our plan."

Eagle took the pipe from his mouth and nodded again. "All right," agreed Blossoms Falling. "He shall not know." Then Blossoms Falling rose. She took an old pouch, poured several hand-fuls of corn kernels into it, then pulled the drawstring closed. She took a piece of fry bread and half a boiled squash and wrapped them in corn husks. "Though you don't ask," she said, "I give. Take this. These are for you and Gaqka."

Grandmother stood. Her shoulders drooped and relaxed. She nodded. She took the offered food and looked quietly at Blossoms Falling and at Eagle. She half-smiled, turned from them, and left their compartment, threading her limping, halting way through the crowded lodge, walking among the many backs turned toward her. Then she was gone.

Eagle turned to Blossoms Falling. He sighed, exhaling a cloud of smoke uneasily. He frowned. "Her son, Ga'no, and I were like brothers. When he disappeared, I thought, these are hard days. Only those who can give to the People are useful. Food is scarce. Enemies lurk." A cloud of gray smoke hid his face. He looked down, pondering. He blew another cloud of smoke from his mouth. "You did right to give her the food," he said.

"You too have done the proper things," said his wife. "Deer meat freezes hard as stone in winter. Still, it cooks up well."

Eagle looked over at her. "Huh," he grunted. So she knew about the meat.

Blossoms Falling continued. "But that old woman has her own ways and can be stubborn. Times have been dangerous. You have hunted. You have protected others. You have driven off enemies and raided too among them. You are neither lazy nor a coward. And now you have offered to help her too."

"Bah," answered Eagle. "I have stood by and taken an easy path. 'Let them grow strong or let them die.' Stupidity! I should have helped them more. That old woman is no fool. She sniffs something on the wind. Tomorrow," he said, "we shall see."

"Tomorrow, then," said Blossoms Falling, once again taking up her deer-jaw scraper and scraping the dried corn kernels from the cob.

Eagle watched the smoke rising from his pipe to mingle with the smoke billowing from the fire. The fire crackled. The smells of burning wood and tobacco joined. The strands of smoke intertwined, rose up, and disappeared through the smoke-hole overhead, out into the night, where stars glittered in the darkness.

Suddenly Raccoon stood grinning before the fire, half-hidden by the smoke. "What's to eat?" he asked.

✦ ✦ ✦

When Grandmother returned, Crow already lay sleeping on his corn husk mat, wrapped in his old, worn robe. She sat beside the dying fire and watched the boy. "Good dreams take you to good roads. But there are things that you do not dream of. Sleep, child. Sleep."

Then Grandmother sat on alone, remembering what had once been in times gone by.

MEN'S TALES

◆ ◆ ◆

CROW rose and stretched. Grandmother was up, poking the fire, adding twigs to make it blaze. *"En-gah-do-went-tah,"* he said. "I am going hunting." He took his bow and quiver of arrows and his knife, put on his moccasins, slung a pouch of cornmeal and maple sugar over his shoulder, and stepped from the lodge. There was a chill in the air, and the clouds were low, as if a roof had been drawn across the Blue, the great dome of the Sky World, where Speaker and Explainer had traveled. The sun sat in a faded glow above the trees.

Crow slipped from the clearing into the forest. He heard a rustling behind him, and there, at a quick pace, came Raccoon, bow in hand, arrows rattling in his quiver, a grin on his broad face.

"Let's go," laughed Raccoon. "I have heard there are lots of big juicy birds deep in the forest. We spies know about such matters. We know the ins and outs of things and how to be useful."

"What do you mean, 'we spies'?" asked Crow.

"Why, me and Skin Man, of course," answered Raccoon mischievously.

Then the two boys set off at a steady pace. Behind them, unseen, three grown warriors — Eagle, Wolf Jaw, and Two Arrows — silently and skillfully stalked their trail. Brother Sun rose higher. After a time he emerged clearly from behind the shifting wall of low gray cloud. Up ahead the boys could see the rounded bulk of Grandfather Stone.

"We come, Grandfather!" called Crow and Raccoon.

"*Dadjoh!* Welcome!" answered the Stone.

Crow laid several finely chipped obsidian arrowheads on the Stone and poured out a mound of cornmeal, a handful of sunflower seeds, and a pinch of sacred tobacco. Then he set down too the deerskin pouch in which he had carried the meal. "I bring gifts, Grandfather," he said, putting down his bow, arrows, and knife and climbing up.

Raccoon put down an arrow of his own beside Crow's gifts and also set a small, flint-bladed knife to which a speckled hawk feather was tied. "I, too, have gifts, Grandfather," he said.

"It is good," said the Stone. "Such good gifts call for stories. Listen, then, for at one time, long ago, it was like this. Back in those early days, before humans arrived, the animals were the People. They could talk . . ."

Crow's face screwed up, and he tilted his head to one side. Then he exclaimed, "But Grandfather, didn't Sky Woman's fall create the earth? Her daughter was born. Then Good-Minded and Hard-Minded. When was there a time before people?"

The Stone answered, "Listen carefully, Grandson. Back then, the story says, the animals were the People. Sky Woman fell, and this earth came into being. But remember, it was Good-Minded who made the People. And both Good-Minded and Hard-Minded were more than human. So there was a time when the animals were the People, before the humans arrived. Who knows how long that time was? Who was there to measure it? What seems short to a stone might seem long to a boy. Does that answer your question?"

Crow shrugged, then nodded.

"So, then," proceeded the Stone, "back in those days Mink was a fierce little fellow but he was clumsy. Grandsons, he would stalk his prey and stumble. Rabbits ran easily from him. It was hard for Mink. Now Mink had a son and he worried about him. *I must catch more food,* Mink thought, *or my poor little boy will never grow big and strong. Aieee. I must hunt well.*

Mink set out looking for food. He smelled a strong rabbit smell. He sniffed and sniffed. It was coming from a tree. He looked up. How could Rabbit climb a tree? he wondered. He didn't know that Raccoon had his nest up there — yes, Raccoon! — and that his nest was lined with rabbit fur! So Mink was sniffing all around. Raccoon heard him.

"Someone's sniffing at my door," said Raccoon. Cautiously

Raccoon peered out from his lodge in the hollow tree and saw Mink sniffing at the base of the tree below, circling all around.

"Ho ho," chuckled Raccoon. "I'll get that Mink."

Raccoon rolled a stone to the door of his tree home. He gave it a shove. Down it fell and *whack,* hit Mink right on the head!

"*Aieeee!*" cried Mink as he ran away, rolling over and over on the ground to ease the sting. Gingerly he touched his head with his paw. It seemed flattened. "My poor head," he groaned, and he hobbled dizzily off along the trail. He found a hollow log and crawled into it and fell asleep. He dreamed that a big rabbit was chasing him, and he twitched and quivered in terror as he dreamed.

Eagle, flying overhead, looked down with his keen eyes."

Wolf Jaw and Two Arrows gripped their war clubs. They looked over from where they were hidden within the bushes toward Eagle, who crouched nearby. Surely the boys had stumbled onto a mystery. The stone, the stone was actually talking! Was it good? Or evil? The two warriors signaled to Eagle, Attack? Eagle shook his head and signed back, Not yet. Stay hidden. Listen. So they stayed put, listening intently.

"He saw the log moving," continued the Stone, "twitching and shaking. Someone is in the log, thought Eagle. Down he swooped and grabbed the log in his strong claws. Beating the air with his great wings, he lifted up again and flew away with the log clutched in his talons, with Mink dreaming in it. Over the forest he flew toward the high mountains, where the nest with his two young eagles in it waited. Whatever is in this log, thought Eagle, will be food for my fledglings. They must be so hungry by now.

Poor Mink. He peered out and — aieeeee! — saw the world swinging below him! He was terrified. At last, with a thump, the log was dropped down into Eagle's nest. "Eat, my children," said Eagle. "Something tasty will come out of this log. Snap it up with your strong beaks. Remember to share." Then Eagle flapped his great wings, lifted up, and was gone, searching for more prey.

Mink heard these words and he shivered with fear. "I'll never go out of this log," he said, determined to survive.

Time went on. Nothing happened. At last Mink could stand it no longer. He peeked out. There were the two fluffy eagle babies rocking together, seated on their big clumsy feet. They saw him and snapped alert — with fear. They backed away from Mink, clicking their beaks and looking for some way to escape.

Why, they're just babies, thought Mink, and suddenly he felt pity for them. He thought of Mink Boy, his poor son. And he shed a tear, thinking he might never see him again.

Mink stepped out of the log. "Don't be afraid," he said. "Look!" and he did a little dance and sang a little song to reassure the eagles. The eagle babies watched. They laughed. Mink smiled. He thought of Mink Boy again and of how hungry he must be. He looked at the eagles. They were hungry too.

He peered down from the nest. There were three mice racing along a narrow rock ledge. Down he leaped, grabbed them, and

then up he climbed again. Two of the mice he gave to the eagle babies. One he ate himself.

After a time the eaglets grew sleepy and began to rock on their big feet, blink their eyes, and doze. Mink crept back into his log and lay there thinking sadly of Mink Boy. Here he was dancing and singing and eating, and poor Mink Boy might have already starved to death! Mink began to really cry now. He made up his mind to climb down from the mountain and cross the valleys and find Mink Boy again. While the young eagles slept he began the difficult descent. It was hard, dangerous work, but at last Mink stood on the ground at the base of the mountain. Then he resolutely set off across the valley. He crossed it, climbed another mountain, descended into the next valley, and went on. Toward sunset he was exhausted. He lay down on a hilltop, turned himself around once or twice, heaved a deep, sad, anxious sigh and, at last, with a great big yawn, fell asleep.

But Eagle was out hunting again. He spied Mink sleeping, swooped down, grabbed him, and brought him back to the nest. The eagle babies cried out, "Oh, Mink is back! Mink is back! We missed him!"

Eagle looked at Mink. "Are you the one who took care of my children?"

"I am," said Mink. "Then I missed my own boy, little Mink. I think he must be very hungry too. But he is so far away. I was going to him when you caught me."

"I will help you," said Eagle.

"You will?" exclaimed Mink, quivering with excitement.

"I will," said Eagle. "First, I'm going to use my power and make you fast, faster than Rabbit."

"Oh, my!" cried Mink with delight.

"I'm going to make you graceful. Your movements will be sure. No enemy will be able to grab you."

"Wonderful!" exclaimed Mink.

"And I'm going to take you back to Mink Boy."

"Hurray!" shouted Mink.

Eagle gave Mink herb medicine to eat. Then he danced around him, waving his wings to cleanse Mink and give him power. Then he took white downy feathers from his own breast and fixed them to Mink's chest, a sign of their friendship.

Then gently Eagle took hold of Mink, flapped his wings, and rose up into the air. He brought Mink back to the very place the log had originally been.

Eagle set Mink down and danced around him one final time in farewell. Then he flapped his wings and flew away.

Mink hurried swiftly, gracefully home.

But Mink Boy was gone. Just then he heard a scuffling sound and looked up. Another mink was coming along, dragging a dead raccoon. Mink's nose wriggled, sniffing the air. He lifted up his head and raced swiftly from the den. "Greetings, stranger," he squeaked. "You seem to be on your way someplace."

"Greetings, stranger," answered the other. "You look hungry. Let's eat together."

The two minks began to eat. Mink paused and asked, "Do you know of a poor starved boy who lives around here?"

"Of course," answered the other between mouthfuls. "I was he."

"But how did you get so big and strong? And how did you become such a good hunter?" asked Mink, astonished.

"I was starving," answered Mink Boy truthfully. "Then one day mice suddenly began to run into my log. I ate them and got strong. Then an eagle flew overhead and dropped roots for me to eat. They had medicine power. For as soon as I ate them I became a skillful hunter. And a fast runner. I can run faster than Rabbit, faster than Fox, faster than Otter. I'm even faster than you now, Father."

"Oh, we'll see about that!" exclaimed Mink. After so much worry he was now bursting with pride, relief, and delight, and he gave his son a great big hug.

"So, way back then, that's how it was," said the Stone. "Now it is finished, a tale of the days when the animals were the People."

Crow said, "I liked it when Mink Boy told about the mice running into his log. Maybe it happened when Mink caught the mice for Eagle's children. I think that is how it was."

"Yeeeeeees. That was good," agreed Raccoon hesitantly. "But I wish it was some other animal that Mink Boy caught — and ate." His lips puckered, and for an instant he almost looked like a big, soft, sad raccoon himself.

Crow said, "Maybe it would have gone better for him if he hadn't dropped that stone onto Mink's head. Still, Raccoon was important. He helped make the world as it is. He gave Mink his flat head."

Raccoon nodded, though doubtfully.

"There is a story with a warrior's heart . . . ," began the Stone quietly. He knew that there were men hiding nearby who were listening. The last story had been to touch them, being a tale of fathers and children. But this would be directly for them, and for the difficulties of the warrior's harsh world of trials and sacrifice and strength that they knew.

"Tell it, Grandfather!" urged the boys, drawn to hear a real warrior's tale.

"Way back, long ago, so far back, it is beyond imagining," said the Stone, "it was like this. *Rumble! Rumble! Clash* and *crash*! The Stone Giants were on the march! Trees were torn and broken in their passing. When they came upon animals or men, they ripped them limb from limb and, with sharp nails and teeth, stripped their flesh from the bones and ate them. They were big and cruel, with skin rough and tough as stone.

Imagine that from the day of your birth you had been rubbed and rolled on rocks and sand. Gradually your skin would become toughened and coarse, and bits of broken rock and sand would work into it. In time a stone coat would cover you head to foot. So it was with these giants. No arrow could penetrate their stone skin.

119

No club or ax or spear — even one hurled by the strongest warrior's arm — could injure them. They were unbeatable.

They had destroyed all the tribes of the north, torn down the lodges, and devoured all the animals and people, making a great wasteland. Then with roars of hunger and pride they set off toward the south. Their marching made the earth shake. Where they passed, desolation and silence lay upon the land. Only the wind moving through the broken trees gave ghostly voice to what had once been—a land rich with animals, forests, and people.

Oh, those giants were fierce. Sometimes they would even turn upon each other and, with thunderous, roaring cries, devour one of their own kind. Their pride was unbounded. "We are great!" they roared. "No one is greater than us! We created ourselves! We stand alone!"

Their cries echoed off the mountains and rose from the earth itself, off old Turtle Mother's shell, all the way up into the Blue. "They have forgotten that all are connected," sighed the Good-Minded Creator. "They forget that one Source flows through all. They are strong, too strong, and have become like a sickness that threatens the land."

The Stone Giants headed steadily south. At night they lodged in caves, but when daylight came they emerged to prowl the forests and catch the unwary. They stormed villages, tearing down the wooden stockades. With stony fists they grabbed the fleeing people and chopped them up in their stony jaws. Brave warriors and old, white-haired, stout-hearted chiefs stood their ground, hurling spears and axes and shooting many sharp arrows. But their efforts were in vain. They died where they stood and the giants marched on unharmed.

In time it seemed that the People would be destroyed entirely and vanish forever from the earth.

Then the Good-Minded Creator sent a messenger to punish the proud giants and save the People. The messenger, Heno, the Thunderer, took the form of a huge Stone Giant, the biggest of all, and descended from the clouds. Then he marched boldly to the entrance of the caves. "I have come," he bellowed, his voice echoing and booming down the stone corridors, "to lead you and be your new chief!"

The Stone Giants assembled and peered out from their caverns. "You may be big," they yelled back, "but what can you do for us? We have already triumphed. Nothing can stand against us. Why should we need you? Go away!"

Then Heno, disguised as the great Stone Giant, motioned with one boulder-like hand. Lightning flashed down and split a nearby mountaintop. He motioned with his other huge fist. *Crack!* A fissure opened in the earth, and flames leaped up.

"You are powerful!" roared the giants in delight. "Yes! Lead us! With you as our chief, nothing can stand against us, not even the Creator. We will overrun the earth. Then we will storm the Sky World!"

"Come down from your caves!" called their new chief. "We march today upon the People. We shall go all together through the long ravine that leads to their biggest settlement on the hilltop. We will tear down the stockade and devour them once and for all!"

"Devour them once and for all!" roared the other giants, descending from the rocky caves and caverns in which they had camped.

Then, with great strides, the army of the Stone Giants set off for the final battle. The earth rumbled and shook beneath their stony feet as on they tramped into the long ravine.

An old man was walking by a lakeside. A crow screamed overhead. He looked up and saw a strange, eerie sight. A bloody human leg dangled in the clouds high overhead. The old man shivered with apprehension. What could this awful vision mean? He sat down beside the lake and watched the clouds reflected in the water's surface. He pointed his mind to the question of his vision. Slowly, a picture formed in the clouds swirling beneath him on the calm surface of the lake. He saw the Stone Giants marching through the long ravine. He heard their war cries. He saw the earth shake. He saw them coming to devour his People.

Shaken, the old man rose and hurried to the village. He told of what he had seen. Warriors gathered and prepared for battle. The people were determined to fight to the last.

A group of warriors went with the old man to the closest end of the ravine. They would act as scouts and see if there might be some way yet to defend the people.

The mighty horde of Stone Giants entered the far end of the long valley. "Stamp!" shouted their new leader, the greatest Stone Giant of them all, as they marched into the valley. "Stamp hard! Stamp harder! Make the earth shake beneath us. We have come to finish the People forever! Make them all quake!" he roared. "Chant loud!" he urged. "Bah! Chant louder! Are we not the mightiest of all? We are the Stone Giants! Let all know of our coming and let all quiver in terror. No one can stand against us. Nothing shall escape! We are the mightiest of all!"

Then how the mighty Stone Giants stamped the ground as they marched. How they roared their wild war chants in great booming voices that made the whole valley echo. Indeed, the earth itself began to shake beneath them. The hills began to tremble. Stones started rolling and tumbling down the steep valley walls. On they marched. On and on. "Louder!" shouted their new leader. "Stronger!"

Louder they chanted. Harder they stamped. Great boulders began to break loose and crash down as the valley narrowed into the ravine. Clouds of dust rose.

"Louder!" roared their leader, the great Stone Giant. "Stamp harder!"

The thundering war cries and terrible stamping march of the

Stone Giants filled the ravine. Dust choked the air. Stones rolled and crashed and bounced down and tumbled. Now all the giants were within the ravine, completely caught up in the power of their own terrible march.

The warriors gathered at the ravine's end heard the unbelievable din. Their ears rang with it. In terror they felt the earth heave and shake. How their hearts pounded with fear. But they gripped their weapons tightly and did not flee. Then, at a sign from their leader, they started forward into the ravine toward the Stone Giants.

The chief of the Stone Giants raised his great boulder-like fists. "Now!" he thundered. "NOW!"

Lightning flashed and suddenly whole sections of the ravine wall broke away and fell down crashing upon the giants. The earth buckled and writhed. Cracks split the ground. Flames leaped. Giants tumbled down, crushed by boulders, by cliffs, and fell helplessly into the flames. Heno, he who had compassionately taken the form of the great Stone Giant, now leaped up himself, the Thunderer once again, in his own true form, and rose up up to the clouds. One Stone Giant alone of all that mighty race escaped from the devastation, fleeing in terror to hide deep in the darkest forest.

The men arrived in time to see and hear it all. Their weapons fell to the ground, and they covered their ears with their hands. Overcome with awe, they sat down slowly upon the trembling ground and gave thanks to Heno and to the Creator who had showed his strength and saved the People.

"All that was long long ago," said the Stone quietly. "Long ago. The giants who seemed so invincible were destroyed by their own pride. The one giant who escaped may still sometimes be found. But he has changed and become good-hearted and humble. That is all. Let us rest now."

The boys looked around and shivered, finding it strange to still see the quiet glade, bright daylight, almost bare trees, and falling leaves. They had half-expected to find mounds of rubble, clouds of dust, piles of gigantic, shattered bones. Hidden among the bushes nearby, Eagle and the two other men, Wolf Jaw and Two Arrows, were thinking of the battles, raids, and losses they had each known — the paths of battle and fierce pride and the many harsh realities of the warrior's life.

DREAM

♦ ♦ ♦

"Sit here, where it is warm, Grandson," said Grandmother, who sat by the fire resewing an old robe. "The night is cold."

Crow entered the lodge and set down a short string of birds. "Bad luck," mumbled Grandmother, eyeing the birds and chewing on a sinew thread to soften it, "changes to good, whatever fools may say and whomever they blame." She took the softened sinew from her mouth and rethreaded the bird-bone-splinter needle. "Winter leads to spring and spring to summer. All comes round again. Here, eat corn soup."

Crow and Grandmother ate. Then Crow took Grandmother's and his own winter moccasins, the ones made of corn straw, and began to stuff them with bird down. Grandmother finished her soup and pushed another length of sinew through the bird-bone needle and resumed her sewing.

"Not too tight," she said to Crow, "or the feathers will stiffen and not warm well. Let there be some space. Don't pack them too tight."

They worked together in silence. The flames crackled. The wind blew, and the fire shuddered and danced. Now Grandmother opened a box containing flattened porcupine quills and began reembroidering the old robe where the quills had torn or been worn away. Crow had finished. The moccasins lay tumbled beside him. He sat up, but his eyes drooped. He began to nod.

"Lie down and sleep," said Grandmother. He lay down and drew his robe over him. He saw Grandmother's face illuminated by the flickering firelight as if embroidered with designs — lines of age and weather crisscrossing her forehead, cheeks, lips, and chin, like patterns of porcupine quills. *It is the face of Grandmother Moon,* thought Crow dreamily. *Craggy and bright.* He listened to the crackling of the fire and to the calling of the wind. Then he tumbled, soft as an armful of feathers, dropping down down into sleep.

He had a dream. He was walking near twilight, heading back to Grandmother and the lodge, a string of birds over his shoulder, when he heard a flapping and croaking from among the bare branches overhead. It was a large crow, balancing cautiously at the tip of a thin branch, using its wings to steady its dark body as it gripped a bare twig with its claws. Gaqka watched as it settled itself, ruffled its feathers, and preened them down. Then it looked at him. "Little Brother," said a dry voice, dry yet tinged with a gentle humor. "Little Brother. It is good you have come."

Gaqka stood still. It was strange. The eye of the crow, so round and black, grew large, grew larger still. Gaqka could see with great clarity. Every detail was sharp, though the light was fading and the crow some distance away. Each downy feather of the ruff around its black beak was as clear to him as if he stood just beside it. He could see too every scale on its dark, slender leg. But still the eye grew larger, until it hung like a round, dark, glistening moon above him. "Come with me," said the voice, so dry and clever and imperious.

It was strange, yet the very strangeness was transparent as water; he was immersed in it, and it hardly impeded him. "But I must find birds for Grandmother," he answered.

The crow chuckled, "Am I not a bird?"

The open, round, luminous black eye, wider still, became a kind of tunnel or den into which Gaqka could walk. He entered.

He was among the branches, looking down at himself, looking down through the crow's eyes at himself standing beneath the trees, still on the trail, looking up. He was and was not Crow. He was himself, yet in some way he was now also standing as a guest within the feathered house of the crow. He heard the beating of the crow's heart like a drum. With a flapping of wings the crow hunched its shoulders and leaped onto the wind. *Flap! Flap! Flap!* They were soaring out over the forest, the wind ruffling along the glossy black feathers. The red sun was marking a brilliant line along the horizon and setting fire to the tops of the distant mountains. The great lake lay huge and glittering. The far-off lands on

the other side of the lake rose faint as a green mist, the forest stretching endlessly into the cold, dark North. The crow turned its head from side to side, and Gaqka could see the curling, flaring wing tips rising and falling on either side. The crow looked down, and Gaqka could see the forest below and the streams touched by the fading light shining like mica. He saw the village, saw Grandmother standing by the old lodge and people, men and women — Jo-ah-Gah, Eagle, Blossoms Falling, Willows Talk, Moons Walking, Flowers Playing, Bear Claw, Wolf Jaw, Two Arrows, Pine Tree Alone — the old chief and others, all walking and talking, laughing and cooking. Men were returning with deer on their shoulders, children and dogs racing to greet them.

They rose higher. He saw many villages, he saw deer and wolf and moose and bear among the trees. At each village smoke rose from cooking fires, hunters returned along the trails, women gathered wood and cooked and scraped skins, and children raced, playing together, sharpening the skills that would help them live and, in time, become the adults of the tribe. They rose still higher. He saw a mountaintop, a cave, and the last Stone Giant, like a pile of stones set on pillars of stone with glowing eyes. He saw . . . he saw . . . Mother! Father! Little Sister!

"Look down," said the crow. "Do you see? This is the great Creation. Here is the greatness of the Creator's world — all the many dreamers, all the many dreams. How can it be comprehended or understood? Look up." Gaqka looked. Clouds unfolded and shifted, turning into fish, serpent, plant, and animal shapes. At the edge of space, at the hinge of day and night, which lay across the far horizon, stars twinkled and shone. And the great Sun Brother, mighty still, flared and blazed his great light like a deep, booming bass voice, like a drum beating and falling upon all things with a warm, vital music, an endless support and encouragement to grow and yet further grow. And Grandmother Moon was lifting her glowing face like a smile, filling the darkness above with her serene presence. Like a cool rain, her light fell too, cooling and gentling, permeating the plant world, raising the sap, drifting like water through the tiniest root hairs and cells, filling the minds of men, animals, birds, with soft, spilling, calm, restful dreams.

It grew darker. Now the countless Star People were shining, winking, and glowing, so that there was no spot, no matter how dark, that was not, at the same time, filled with light.

"Lift your voice. There are ways and ways and ways. The worlds are endless. Paths without limit. Find your way and trust, even as the falling leaves trust when they drift down, turning this way and that. So the countless changes of a life endlessly come. Now we see one side, now another. *Gaa gaa! Gaa! Gaa! Gaa GAA!*"

Crow awoke with that laughing call still echoing raucously in his mind. The sound of crow calls came too from the trees outside the lodge. Closer they sounded, then farther off, then they were gone. *GAA! Gaa!* He lay on his mat, smiling in gratitude for the encouragement and blessing his namesake, Crow, had brought him in a dream. He was on the right Path.

The day brightened. Grandmother rose and stirred up the fire, adding twigs and blowing on the embers until the flames rose and crackled. Crow rose and took his bow and quiver, filled his pouch with parched corn and maple sugar. "I will go now, Grandmother. I will hunt birds."

"May it go well with you, Grandson," answered Grandmother. "May the day go happily."

That night the men had been troubled, yet strangely elated too, as they returned to the village. They felt energized, as if they had been in the presence of some good power, some strong *orenda*. It had been, they admitted, confusing, for, if that was so, it seemed as if this outcast orphan boy, Crow, the one everyone blamed for recent mishaps, might be the power's messenger.

Yes, following Crow had changed everything. It was as if an old stone ax or maul had been lifted, turned in the hand, and . . . an entirely new shape and function was suddenly revealed. It was that simple and that strange. Hidden in the bushes, listening to the stories, none of them had dared step forward to confront the boys and . . . and what? . . . a talking stone? Why? What had stopped them, frozen them in their places so? After all, they were warriors, grown men who had faced death and danger for the tribe's sake many times. But this was different and totally unsettling. Yet two untried boys — one of them Eagle's own son — had sat and calmly listened, unafraid.

"That was what we heard, wasn't it?" asked Wolf Jaw as they came back along the trail. "I . . . just want to be sure we agree. It was a boulder that . . . lived. That talked."

The others nodded. "Not only did it talk," admitted Two Arrows, "it talked so well, I didn't want to interrupt. I didn't want the spell it wove to break. I wanted only to listen."

"What will the old woman say when we tell her?" muttered Eagle. "We'll be shamed."

Two Arrows cleared his throat and said, "Let's just tell her that we trailed her grandson and Jo-ah-Gah, and that birds were really scarce. Yet we will add that we plan to follow them again tomorrow. We still think there's more to it. Some power, but one not *otgont*, may be behind it. The sudden scarcity of birds touches a greater mystery."

Eagle nodded, as did Wolf Jaw. "Tomorrow, then," said Eagle. "Meanwhile, your words are good. I will do what I can to persuade the old woman of this supposed plan. Meanwhile, Gaqka and Jo-ah-Gah must know nothing. In the morning we three will return to follow them and the trail of this Storytelling Stone — wherever it may lead. If the path turns toward evil, we must be prepared to fight it to the death. We will need fire. What else could harm a stone? Agreed?"

The others nodded. "Agreed."

"Everyone carry an ax and flints," said Wolf Jaw. "We'll cut brush and wood, start a fire, and heat it till it cracks if we have to."

STORIES

◆ ◆ ◆

CROW left the old lodge and entered the forest, walking confidently forward, suspended still between the world of his dream and the bright, daytime world around him. Soon he heard footsteps approaching. It was Raccoon. At a trot they set off in single file along the trail that led deeper into the forest. The sun rose higher and shone down through the trees. Behind them came the men — Eagle, Wolf Jaw, Two Arrows, and also Two Arrows's brother, the young warrior called Fist, who had insisted on coming along too. The Moon of Falling Leaves was almost over. A few brown shriveled leaves still clung to the bare branches like emptied cocoons. Here and there masses of red or orange leaves still flamed majestically.

The clearing in which Grandfather Stone rested soon lay before them.

"We have come, Grandfather!"

"Welcome," answered the Stone.

Crow and Raccoon placed gifts on the Stone — sacred tobacco, dried corn, pouches of corn pollen.

"Sit down. I have stories," said the Stone. "Constancy is a virtue. Sometimes children fulfill destinies begun in the past. It can take time to complete the whole story. There are cycles that time unfolds and reveals. You see, once there were two brothers. One was named Younger and the other Driven. The boys were bold and liked adventurous games. There were two hills near where they lived. Driven liked to go to the summit of the one and, with a mighty leap, soar to the summit of the other. Younger would stand in the valley between and shoot an arrow at him as he jumped. No arrow could hurt Driven. They all missed or bounced off, leaving him unharmed. But there was one arrow their grandmother had warned them never to shoot. "It belonged to your father," she would say. "Never, never shoot that one."

When the boys were still young they would whisper to each other, "It is forbidden," eyeing their father's arrow warily. But as they grew older they would discuss it and say, "Why not shoot Father's arrow? What can be the harm in that?"

One day they took the arrow and began their game of leaping and shooting again. Driven leaped. Younger shot. The arrow struck. And this arrow, their father's arrow, pierced Driven through the chest and carried him off, out of sight.

Younger threw himself down on the ground and wept bitter tears, sobbing, "I have killed my own brother."

Then at last Younger rose, wiped his eyes, and set off after Driven, determined to find and save his brother, if he still lived, or to die trying himself.

Younger trudged on through dark nights and weary days. Finally, up ahead, he saw a lump on the ground. He ran forward. There, pinned to the earth by the arrow, but still just barely alive, was his brother, Driven. Younger pulled the arrow from the earth, freeing his wounded brother. He brought berries and water for Driven, then lifted his injured brother up on his own back. Driven was terribly weak, but he raised a thin hand and pointed north. "That way, Brother," he whispered. "It is the way we must go. What has happened has opened a new trail for us. With the eyes of my wounding, I see it. We must go forward, not back. Our healing now lies this way."

Dutifully Younger set off with Driven upon his back. Driven's eyes seemed to look into the Other World, so close was he to death. He could see things that others could not. He said, "Ahead there is a house with many women dancing in it. We will come to it. Do not doubt this. The women will be very pretty, but we must not look upon them, Brother. To pass safely we must not look. If we do look, we will remain trapped in that house forever."

"I will not look," said Younger as on he walked to the north.

In time they heard women's voices singing. Now they heard the echoes of feet dancing. Then lovely voices called, "Come in, come in. Look at us! Behold us! We are beautiful!"

Younger trudged on, his eyes fixed on the ground ahead.

After a time, Driven spoke again: "Alas. There is another danger. If we pass through, we will be safe and able to return home. Ahead there are women who are making a quilt of men's eyes. The eyes they have taken blink and look and live. The eyes open and shut, looking this way and that. It is a quilt of living eyes. If we can pass through the lodge without looking at that quilt, we will be safe. But, Brother, if we look, our eyes will at once be added to the quilt and we will wander in darkness. Be prepared. It will not be easy. The quilt is fascinating, hard to resist. In the lodge it will be overpowering. It will be what we want to look at most. All else will seem as nothing."

They came to the lodge. Younger bent low as they went within, so that only the ground was before his eyes. It was all he saw. Then a woman's voice said, "Look up! Look up! Do not bend so low. Ah, the quilt is beautiful. It likes to be looked at. It would look at you. Stand up and look. It is a sight not to be missed. See the beautiful Quilt of Eyes!"

Younger trudged doggedly on, his eyes fixed on the ground. They were almost safely through and just about to exit the lodge at its far side when a woman ran before them and waved the quilt before them. Then Younger SAW. At once his eyes jumped from their sockets and leaped onto the quilt. The world went dark. Younger stumbled through the door. Driven, in a sudden burst of life, leaped from his brother's shoulders and ran off, crying, "We are through! Run!"

But Younger could not see. He crept forward on his hands and knees, blind. Driven was gone.

Younger crawled on, blind and alone. Over rocks and stones, through streams, into bushes and brambles. Finally he came to a field of corn. He crept among the tall plants, their leaves *swooshing* and swinging in the breeze. He curled up there and slept. He stayed there, hoping that when someone came to care for the plants they would find him. He could crawl no farther.

A day went by. Then another. Then Younger heard a woman's voice sweetly singing as she walked among the corn. The beauty of her voice took the pain and grief momentarily away. He called out to her. The voice stopped. Footsteps approached. Then he heard a gasp of surprise and the footsteps ran off, pattering among the corn like faint rain, and were gone. Younger had never felt so alone.

The young woman ran on until she came to the lodge in which she lived with her older sister. "A man," she panted, "a man with no eyes is lying among the corn plants. He looks so tired. His clothes are torn. His hands and knees are raw and bloodied."

"We must help him," said the older sister. "He needs help. We cannot just leave him. We shall bathe his wounds and give him good food until he is well."

The two sisters returned together. Younger heard their footsteps approaching, and his heart beat with expectation. "Do not be afraid," said the older. "We will help you," said the younger. "Stand now. You have our shoulders to lean on. We will guide you to our lodge. We have food there, and you can rest."

So Younger returned with them to their lodge. They fed him on bear oil and corn soup, on fry bread, venison, and squash. They made him well, and when his strength was renewed and he had good clothes on again, they asked how he had come to be in such a pitiable condition.

Then Younger said, "I shot my brother with a forbidden arrow left us by our father. I was carrying him to safety through a house of witches. Then one witch shook the Quilt of Eyes before me. I saw the eyes blinking and flashing; some looked bold, others fearful. That was the last sight I saw. All went dark. My eyes were gone, sewn with the others dangling on that horrible quilt. My wounded brother escaped, and I crawled on to rest at last in your cornfield, where you found me. I do not know what became of my poor brother, and I hope, still, to find him. I have vowed to restore him while life remains."

The sisters pitied Younger. In their care he daily grew stronger. Though blind, he chopped wood and carried branches and fished; he wove splint baskets and carved digging tools and spoons and ladles. And he told the sisters of his life.

One day the younger sister and Younger spoke words of love to each other. In time they decided to marry. So Younger married the younger sister, and they settled in together with the older sister in the lodge where the two girls had lived so long alone.

It was a good life. They were good companions. About a year later Younger's wife gave birth to twin boys. The first to be born they named Thistle, and the next, Last. Younger gave thanks for the birth of his children.

But those boys were strange. They talked together in a language of their own. Then they asked for a lacrosse stick and ball. They began to play. They played through the house. They went outside and played. They went into the ground under the house and played. When they emerged they were already half-grown. Then they asked for bows and arrows. When they got them, they went off for days, then returned. "More monsters are gone from this earth," they laughed when they returned. They were grown now. Oh, they grew fast.

Now that they were grown, they went to their father and asked, "Where are your eyes? What happened to them? Tell us. There are things we might do."

So Younger told them the story of the Quilt of Eyes and of the disappearance of his brother, Driven.

Then the boys said, "Father, we will get your eyes back."

"Do not go!" exclaimed Younger. "It is dangerous. I know. I went there and just look what happened!"

Then the boys looked at each other and laughed. They went out and began to play. Soon they returned. But Younger could not understand what they were speaking about. For they said, "Hang on! Hang on! We are almost back to where Father is. He will help us."

Then they took their father by the hand and guided him forward. He touched a body. It was warm. It lived. But it was very thin. An arrow protruded from its chest. No eyes were in its eye sockets. "Driven!" cried Younger. "Oh, my brother! But you have lost your eyes too!"

And the body answered, "Younger! My brother! Yes, I saw the quilt too! Oh, it is true!"

And the two men reached out blindly and grasped each other.

The children said, "Oh, you need eyes. You should see one another!" and off they ran. They went into the forest and they found a fawn. She stood still, wide-eyed, petal ears out to each side, poised for flight as they approached. But they stopped and called out so gently, "Little fawn! little fawn!" that she let them approach. Then the boys said, "Sweet fawn, let us borrow your eyes. They are so beautiful, dark, with curled lashes. We will return them and bring you good mushrooms, and leaves and berries to nibble. We promise to do you no harm. It is only to help our father, who yearns now to see his poor brother. Oh, it is pitiful! Their eyes have been stolen, and they are blind."

The fawn said, "You may take my eyes. I will wait here. Return them soon."

So the boys gratefully took the fawn's eyes and, leaving her a pile of soft moss to eat while they were gone, hurried back to the lodge.

They brought the eyes to their father and placed them in his empty sockets. He saw his children. He wept for joy, for they were handsome and good. He saw his poor brother, so thin and streaked with earth.

"Ah, Driven," he exclaimed, "how old, how like Father, almost, you now look!" Then he gazed and gazed, gazed like a man who has been thirsty a long time and is given water at last. He gazed on the sun and trees, on his wife and sister-in-law and sons. "But it is not fair," he said then. "Driven must see too." Then the boys took the eyes and placed them in Driven's empty sockets. Driven now looked upon his tall nephews, upon his brother, Younger, upon his sister-in-law, and upon her older sister. He too gazed and gazed.

Then the boys took the eyes. "We must bring these back to that good fawn," they said. "We will get your eyes now. But," they laughed, "they will not be as pretty as these. Your lashes will not be half as long!"

They returned the eyes to Fawn and brought her good leaves and berries and soft mushrooms and moss. With her eyes back in place, Fawn looked at the food and at the twins. She smiled.

The boys journeyed on to the house of the Quilt of Eyes. When they saw it ahead they sat down in the bushes and planned their attack. They went to the spring. Last changed himself into a duck that swam and bobbed on the surface, round and round. Thistle hid among the long grasses by the shore. Then one of the witches came down to the spring. Last sprang out from his duck form and became a bit of down, floating on the breeze. The down became a tiny seed drifting almost unseen on the air. The witch yawned and swallowed the seed.

Not long after that, the woman gave birth to a child, a boy. The child cried and cried. Whatever they gave it was no good. It just cried and cried. At last they grew so weary of its lusty crying, one of the witches said, "Let it play with the quilt. Maybe that will pacify it. I want to sleep!" The child was given the quilt. The eyes on the quilt opened and closed, turned and flashed, winked and blinked. The child cooed and laughed. The weary witches, pleased, fell asleep at last. Then the child stood up. It was Last. Holding the quilt tight, he ran. The witches awoke. They tried to kill him with clubs. But he was fast. He dodged and turned. They lashed and struck. They hit each other. Hard. That was the end of them.

Thistle rose from among the weeds. Together, the twins set off for home. When they arrived, their mother ran to greet them. In their hands the quilt was safe to look at. They showed her the quilt. They took it inside. "Father," they asked, "what were your eyes like?"

"Well," he answered, scratching his head, remembering, "they were like yours."

The boys looked at the quilt. They found a pair like their own eyes. They took them and put them in their father's sockets. He jumped up and did a dance and cried aloud in joy, "I can see!"

He looked at the quilt. "Those, those there are Driven's eyes — right there!" he exclaimed.

They took the eyes. They put them in the sockets. Now Driven jumped up and cried, "I can see!" The two brothers embraced.

The boys said, "So many eyes. We must bring the dead to life and give them back their eyes. How can we be happy when so many suffer? Poor dead ones. Poor flashing eyes with no sockets."

They went back to the witch-lodge with their father and uncle. They found many graves there. They dug up the bones, half as many skulls as eyes. They built a sweat lodge and placed the jumbled bones in there. It got warm. The air began to quiver. The lodge began to shake. The boys pushed over an elm tree, shouting, "Come on, bones! Come on out and live!" Then the skeletons arose in panic, arms and legs all tangled, skulls dropping. They grabbed. They reset arms and legs and backs and skulls and poured out from the lodge into the glorious eye-bright day! They had bodies again, and flesh. The people lived. They laughed and called out in joy.

But the twins had worked too fast. The skeletons had been too hurried. Some were short, and some tall. Some wide, and some narrow. And some were all mixed-up. Everyone was different that might have been the same. They couldn't go back to where they had come from. The heads and arms and legs might all be from different places. So the world became what it is today: a bit mixed-up, a bit mixed together.

That was all right with the twins. They just paced out the site of a large lodge. Like magic, it sprang up where they had paced. "Here's a place for you," they called. "Live here, near us. We will be one people."

Driven, the boys' uncle, had his eyes now, and with those eyes, he could clearly see what a beauty the boys' aunt was. He had his health too for the two sisters had been feeding him well. And the wound in his chest was healed.

Driven and the older sister were married. Then the two couples and all the people and the mighty twins lived on in the forest. Of course, sometimes the twins traveled and did great deeds. But always they returned home again.

So the story goes. There are many such adventurous stories. In them, anything is possible. Yet many painful things can happen on the way to that good, happy ending, the ending that all seek. Let me show you what I mean. But first, tell those who are hidden to step into the open like grown men. Warriors should not skulk so."

"What do you mean, Grandfather?" stammered Crow, looking around.

"Those that hear, know. Tell them it is time. Tell them to come out, put down their axes and flints, and listen."

Crow looked at Raccoon and shrugged. He stood up on the Stone, put his hands to his mouth, and called, "Grandfather Stone says come out from hiding. Join us and listen openly like men!"

For a moment all was silent. Then, from nearby, came a rustling of bushes. Eagle rose, as did Wolf Jaw, Two Arrows, and Fist.

"Father!" exclaimed Raccoon, shocked.

Eagle nodded uneasily. The men gripped their weapons and looked quite uncomfortable to have been found out. How had the Stone known of their presence? And now to be exposed by this thing of power! The boys could not understand how nakedly revealed the men felt. Their own skill and power had been stripped from them. They felt vulnerable as children. The Stone had even spoken of their axes and flints.

Then Raccoon turned to Crow and laughed — "More spies! Your grandmother has been busy."

Even the men grinned ruefully at that.

"Come," said the Stone. "It is time. You have been listening well. Now you shall openly hear stories of the Long-Ago Time. No more hiding. The stories have good power. This is what draws and silences you. It is not *otgont*. You need not fear. Put down your weapons and come close. This will bring good to you and your people. You will be among the first men in this world to know the old ways and tales."

The men looked at each other and at Eagle. They nodded. Reluctantly they released their grip on their weapons and set down their bows and knives and clubs. Then they cleared some of the brush from around the Stone and seated themselves.

"Set a few gifts on me," said the Stone. "Stories should be respected and paid for."

The men then rose and each placed something — a knife, an ax, a pouch of flints, an arrow — on the Stone beside the boys' gifts. Then, when they were seated again, the Stone began. "Let it be like this. Long ago, back when the world was infested with powerful sorcerers, there were two brothers living with their uncle. These weren't twins. No. The older boy's name was Two Feathers. The younger was named Turkey Brother."

Crow and Raccoon looked at each other and raised their eyebrows.

"There are many tales of Turkey," said the Stone, pausing. "In this one, he is young. There are other tales of Two Feathers too. But as I now say, they lived together in a lodge. They lived alone because the people of their village had been overcome by the evil sorcerers and all were now gone. Only the uncle and the two boys lived on.

Two Feathers was almost a man now. Turkey was still a boy. Turkey asked his older brother to get him a turkey skin.

"Why?" asked Two Feathers.

"Oh, I just feel I should be wearing that," answered the boy offhandedly. Two Feathers knew that Turkey was asking for something with power for him. He hunted and brought him a turkey skin. The boy slipped into it. He looked like a turkey. He ran around and gobbled, sounding like a turkey. He flapped his arms and rose to the treetops and perched there like a turkey. He was no ordinary child.

The old uncle said to Two Feathers, "Now you should prepare

for manhood. Go to the river. Fast, build a sweat lodge, and purify yourself. Protectors will appear to you. No matter how strange they look, trust them. They will have come to help you."

Two Feathers went to the river. He fasted. He built a small sweat lodge with bent willow branches covered with skins. He made a fire, heated rocks till they glowed, poured on water and prayed and purified his mind within the little lodge. A giant spider appeared. It seemed to be descending on a cord from the treetops. "When you are in trouble and danger, when you need a friend, I will come and protect you," it said. Then it was gone. A great black snake appeared. "If you are in danger, in trouble and distress," it hissed softly, "I will come and help you. You are not alone. I too am your protector."

Two Feathers knew his protectors. He knew now that he was not alone in this world and that guardians who meant him only good would stand by him. He emerged from the sweat lodge and gave thanks to the unseen powers. He returned to his uncle.

The old man looked at Two Feathers and smiled. "Nephew," he said, "it seems to me that you are now a man. Your protectors have revealed themselves. It is time to find a wife. You will have to journey to find her, as our own people are gone. To the east is a chief with daughters. Go there. Yes, it will be good to have someone who is clear-minded and who can really cook come to live with us, someone who can make this old lodge a home.

"You will need the right clothes. A wife must see your splendor.

And it is a long journey, I am thinking. You will need good clothes. Let me see what will be the best clothing for you."

The uncle bent down and pulled a bark box out from under the low, shelf-like bed built into the side of the lodge. He lifted the lid of the box and drew out a beautiful robe of raccoon skin. The fur was soft and smooth. Raccoon ears stood out on the side of the head. "Put it on, Nephew."

Two Feathers put it on. The old man circled round him, looking carefully, pursing his lips. He shook his head. He sighed. "No, you don't look good enough," he said. "You will not find the right wife in this. Take it off."

Two Feathers took off the robe. The uncle folded it back up. Then he lifted out another robe. This one was of wildcat skin and hung down in a fringe of tails. There were ears sewn onto the shoulders and eyes on the sleeves. "Put this one on, Nephew."

Two Feathers eagerly put it on. It felt powerful. His senses felt keen. He could see even in areas of shadow. He heard the buzz of a wasp circling outside the lodge. The uncle circled, examining Two Feathers. "This is an old robe, Nephew. It has magic. It is cunning. The ears and eyes are alert and will protect the man who wears this shirt." He circled again, pausing to look carefully. "Nooo," he sighed at last, shaking his head slowly back and forth. "There are dangers on the path you must take, and the wife who awaits at journey's end is a discerning young woman. These clothes are not yet good enough."

Reluctantly Two Feathers took off that fine shirt. Shadows deepened in the lodge. His eyes seemed to grow dim. He heard only the movements of his uncle beside him as he folded the wildcat shirt.

The uncle bent down and lifted a deerskin case from the box. Carefully he opened the flap of the case and drew out another shirt. He unfolded it. It was a shirt of panther skin with a hood of a panther's neck and a cap of its head. The ears were erect. The eyes perched on the face of the hood. Two tall heron feathers stood at the top of the cap. "Put this one on, Nephew."

Two Feathers put on the panther shirt. His arms felt strong, and his heart was without fear. He could hear the wasp circling outside. He could hear the ants crawl. The shadows disappeared. Even the darkest corners of the lodge were bright as day. His mind felt clear.

"Hmmm," said the uncle, circling around him, looking. The uncle stopped walking. He bent down. He took out a pair of wildcat leggings. "Put these on, Nephew."

Two Feathers put them on. His legs felt strong. He felt that he could now run tirelessly all through the day. "Hmmm," said the uncle, circling Two Feathers and stroking his chin thoughtfully. "Hmmm." He took out a pair of moccasins. "Put these on, Nephew."

Two Feathers put them on. He could feel the earth spreading beneath his feet. The earth held him up and gave him strength. "Take these, Nephew." And the uncle handed Two Feathers a pouch of fisher-skin with a fisher-head on the flap. Two Feathers slung it on. The uncle gave him a pouch of spotted fawn-skin with the hoofs dangling down. Two Feathers slung it on. He handed him an old bow, a quiver of arrows, and a clay pipe with the face of a bear on it and with snakes. Two Feathers took them. The uncle circled.

"The heron feathers will speak and warn you of danger," said the uncle, standing before him. "In these moccasins you will travel fast in long, leaping strides. You will feel like you are skimming over the earth. With them on your feet, a journey of many days will be finished in less time than our Brother Sun takes to rise to his midday house in the Blue. The fisher-skin pouch is alive. Should anyone reach out to harm you, even while you sleep, it will bite them. In the pouch is a medicine root. One end is dark, the other light. Chew the dark end and dark wampum will flow from your mouth. From the light end will pour white wampum. The bear on the pipe will come alive when you smoke. It will growl when an enemy touches it. The snakes will hiss. The fawn-skin pouch is alive. It will be a companion. The bow looks old and weak, but it has the power of age and will guide every arrow wisely to the target. Shoot with it and you cannot miss. Oh, you look good, Nephew. This shirt is the right one. Now you are ready."

Two Feathers could hardly wait to set out. But the uncle said, "Wait, Nephew, do not be hasty. Let me give you some advice. Listen carefully. The path ahead is filled with dangers. There are evil sorcerers lying in wait for the unwary. This is how it will be. There will be a clearing, and in it a boy will be playing. 'Lift me from the ground,' he will cry to you, begging so pitifully. 'Lift me up so I can swing on this branch overhead.' Do not listen, Nephew! He is the creation of a sorcerer who hides in the tree. Should you lift the boy the sorcerer will grab you, tie you to an arrow, and shoot you far off to his lodge, where an evil witch waits to cook you over the fire. No, just walk on, Nephew, and pay no attention to the boy. Farther on you will come to a spring. You will be thirsty. The spring is deep, the water cold as ice. Monsters live in the spring, and should you bend to drink, they will grab you with powerful arms and draw you in. Be careful, Nephew! Stay alert! Finally, as you come close to the village you seek, you will see a grove of tall trees. An old man will be among those trees, hopping around this way and that. He will beg you to shoot a raccoon for him, saying that he is old and weak and hungry. His pleas will be heartrending for one as kind as you. Do not trust him, Nephew! He will be your ruin! Walk on and do not be deceived, for that one's heart is rotten, hollow as an old tree. Follow my advice, Nephew, and all will be well. These are my words to you. Heed them."

Then Two Feathers thanked his uncle and prepared to set out. Turkey Brother began to cry, "Take me, too, I should go! I am ready!"

"No," said the uncle. "You are young."

"No," said Two Feathers. "I journey alone."

But Turkey cried out, "Take me! I will help you! Take me! I will remember Uncle's warnings!" He flapped his arms like a turkey and gobbled loudly.

At last Uncle said, "All right."

And Two Feathers said, "If you are ready, we will go now!"

"I'm ready!" laughed Turkey, slipping into his turkey skin. "You will soon see just how ready I am."

Then, saying farewell to their uncle the two boys set out. Oh, but it was wonderful how those powerful boys traveled! Turkey flew ahead from tree to tree, gobbling and calling to mark the trail. Two Feathers strode along after at such a pace it was almost as if he were flying himself. The distance they traveled in only a few days would have taken ordinary people weeks to traverse.

After a time they came to a clearing. A boy was playing there, leaping and jumping and tossing small sticks like spears. He called, "Welcome! Come, help me get up into this tree. Lift me up!"

Turkey gobbled loudly, warning Two Feathers. Two Feathers came close to the boy. "I'll help," he said. Then he grabbed the boy and, rather than standing on a stump below the branches of the tree himself and lifting the boy up, put the boy on a stump instead. At once two great arms reached down — they had been disguised as branches — and with a roar like the rushing of the wind in the treetops, the stump was lifted up, fixed to the tip of an arrow and shot through the air. Off it flew, and in an instant, it was gone from sight. Far away it came down through the smoke-hole of a lodge and knocked the witch waiting there right into the fire, ending her cruel life. Only a cloud of ashes remained. At once the boy — an illusion created by the hidden sorcerer — disappeared. The sorcerer himself was locked in the tree forever, his arms now truly branches, his power spent.

Turkey flapped his wings, gobbled in joy, and flew ahead. Two Feathers strode rapidly after. After a time they came to a spring bubbling up out of the earth. Turkey gobbled, "Remember our uncle's warning, Brother!"

Dutifully they walked on. Then Two Feathers stopped. "I'm thirsty," he said. He turned back and returned to the spring. Turkey gobbled and gobbled. But Two Feathers knelt and drank. Two powerful, hairy arms reached out of the water, gripped Two Feathers, and began to pull him down. Two Feathers pulled back mightily. With a great heave he flung the creature out of the water and onto the grass, where it lay on its back, kicking the grass furiously with its heels, screaming, "Put me back in the water!" Two Feathers called out, "Keep watch over it, Turkey. Don't let it return." Turkey stood over the monster. Its struggles grew weaker and weaker. Then it was still.

Again, Two Feathers drank. But again a hairy monster reached up and grabbed him. Two Feathers pulled that monster out too. Then once more he drank. A monster grabbed. But Two Feathers prevailed this time too, pulling the creature from the water and tossing it onto the grass. At last all three monsters lay still. The water bubbled higher and clearer than ever. Then Two Feathers and Turkey knelt down and drank from the clear spring. Once a village had stood here. But when the monsters entered the spring they had destroyed the people. Now their evil ways were done.

Turkey flapped his wings and flew on. Two Feathers came striding rapidly after. They came to a grove of tall trees. There was an old man there leaping about, hopping first on one foot, then on the other. "Help me! Help me, Nephews!" he called. "There is a raccoon up on a branch overhead. I have no bow or arrow to shoot it with and I am so hungry. Oh, shoot, shoot it for me!"

Turkey began to gobble a warning, but Two Feathers said, "Of course I will shoot it for you, Uncle." Turkey gobbled loudly. But Two Feathers strung his old bow, raised an arrow to the string, and shot. *Zzzzzzt!* The arrow struck. The raccoon tumbled from the branch down into a hole in the tree, which was hollow.

"Oh, no, no!" cried the old man, hopping this way and that in agitation. "I am too old to climb. I will starve still. Oh, get it, climb up and get it for me, Nephew!"

"I will do that, Uncle," said Two Feathers, who set down his bow and quiver of arrows, ready to climb.

"Wait, Nephew," said the old man, growing suddenly calm. "Your clothes are beautiful. Take them off, lest you ruin them. This old tree has many snags, and the bark is rough and dirty. I will guard your fine clothes."

Turkey gobbled and gobbled a warning. But Two Feathers took off his fine panther shirt with its hood and its heron feathers. He took off his wildcat leggings and his fleet moccasins and his fisher-skin pouch and his spotted fawn pouch with the dangling hoofs. Then he took hold of a branch, swung himself up, and climbed swiftly to the top. Oh, it was easy. He was young and strong. He was just reaching into the hollow tree when something came up behind him and pushed. Hard. He tumbled down down down into the depths of the hollow tree. He felt bare bones crunch beneath his feet. The face of the old man peered down from the opening, now high above. Two Feathers called out to him, "Help me out, friend!"

"Good-bye!" sneered the old man.

From outside the hollow tree, Two Feathers could hear Turkey gobbling and calling and shrieking loudly, a sign that something bad was taking place. Two Feathers tried and tried to get out, but the inside of the tree was smooth, and he could not get a grip. Men's bones crunched and clicked together beneath him. He stood on a pile of old, dry bones.

The old sorcerer climbed down. He took off his old, filthy, torn clothes. He put on the panther shirt, the good leggings, the fleet moccasins. He slung on the fisher pouch and the fawn pouch. When he put them on, he looked young, not like an old man at all. "I don't need that crooked old, worm-eaten bow," he said disdainfully. "I can get a much better one in the village ahead. I shall marry the girl waiting there for Two Feathers. I shall trick them all just as I tricked him."

Then, the now young-looking Imposter, becoming more handsome with each step, set off through the trees. Soon he was gone. The sun began to set. The sky grew dark. Turkey flew into the treetops and gobbled for help. But no one came.

All night long Two Feathers tried to escape from that place of terror and death. But all his efforts failed, no matter how hard he tried. At last, dawn's gray light shone down into the tree. Two Feathers was exhausted. He now feared that his own bones would soon be added to the pile of whitened bones already there. He felt sad for all those who had been tricked and trapped like he was now. He felt sad for all who had died there. At that moment, as he thought of others, suddenly he remembered his protectors and he called out, "Come, friend Spider! Help me! I am in danger!"

Giant Spider appeared overhead and dropped a silken line to Two Feathers. Two Feathers took the cord, and the great spider pulled him up and up. He was almost out when the cord broke. Down fell Two Feathers with a crash, back down onto the bones. Spider said, "I am sorry, Grandson. My strength is not great enough." Then it was gone.

Two Feathers painfully stood up again. "Come, Black Snake," he called desperately. "I need your help."

Black Snake appeared and let its tail down into the tree. Two Feathers took hold of the end, which coiled firmly about him. The snake pulled its tail back up, raising Two Feathers safely to the opening. Two Feathers climbed out. He thanked the snake, which disappeared. Then Two Feathers climbed back down the tree to where Turkey was waiting.

The old man's old, torn, filthy garments lay in a pile where Two Feathers's beautiful clothes had been neatly placed. Gingerly, Two Feathers slipped on the dirty old clothes. He put on the stiff moccasins and the torn, rotted cap with bedraggled feathers. His beauty faded. He became wrinkled and weak and old. Leaning on Turkey, who gobbled softly, encouragingly, he set off like an old, sick man, walking slowly in those foul clothes toward the village.

When the Imposter wearing Two Feathers's fine clothes got to the river, he called across in a strong, clear, young voice, "I am Two Feathers. Bring me across."

The chief's older daughter heard that call. She pushed a canoe into the river and paddled across. The Imposter got in, and as they paddled back, he said proudly, "I am a great hunter. I am young and handsome. I have many gifts to offer and I have many powers. I am looking for a wife."

The chief's older daughter said, "I would like such a husband. Let us go to my father together."

They went to the chief. The Imposter boldly said, "I come as your son-in-law." The chief looked at the fine panther shirt, the wildcat leggings, the beautiful moccasins, the fine pouches. He saw strength and vigor and wealth. He saw his oldest daughter's smiling face. "Welcome, Son-in-Law," he said.

That night, the old Imposter ate wedding bread and was married to the oldest daughter of the chief. He went to her place in the lodge, an alcove curtained with fox skins, a bed covered with soft pelts and furs. But even there, he would not take off his fine, stolen clothes.

In the morning, Two Feathers and Turkey came to the river. Two Feathers called across in a hoarse, weak whisper of a voice, "Will someone carry us across the river?"

The Imposter heard and said, "Don't go. It is just a sick old man and a turkey."

But the chief's youngest daughter said, "Who are you to tell us what to do? I go when someone calls for aid." She paddled across. Turkey helped Two Feathers into the canoe. The woman marveled that a turkey would help a man. Two Feathers said, "He is not a turkey. He is my brother. I am not an old man. I am a young man. My name is Two Feathers, and I am seeking a wife."

The girl looked at him. She said, "If you are a young man, you are the oldest young man I have ever seen! How can you be young?"

Two Feathers told her.

The chief's youngest daughter was quiet for a time when she heard his tale. Then she said, "I think some of those bones you speak of are the bones of my lost brothers. I believe you and I will help."

When they were across she took Two Feathers's hand. She led him slowly to her father's lodge. She stood before her father, the chief, with Two Feathers, looking so old and bent, wearing old torn, dirty clothes beside her. "I have brought my husband," she boldly announced. The Imposter said, "What! Should a fine, young girl marry an old, broken-down wretch? Forbid it!"

The chief looked at the Imposter. He looked calmly at his daughter. "My daughter knows her own mind," he said. "Welcome, Son-in-Law."

Then the girl led Two Feathers to her place in the lodge, an alcove with curtains of soft doeskin. The bed was beautiful, covered with soft robes and furs. The skin walls and ceiling were embroidered with porcupine quills forming patterns of flowers and stars. Good herbs hung there, making the place sweet and clean and fresh. "The shelf overhead shall be a place for Turkey to rest," she said.

That night, Two Feathers ate marriage bread. Only the chief welcomed him. No one else even spoke to him. He was old and sick-looking. He would only be another mouth for the hunters to feed. What good could he be to the People?

"Come," laughed the Imposter, "let that old wreck munch marriage bread with soft, toothless gums. It is shameful, disgusting. Come over here, I say, and I will show you just a few of my many wonders." Eagerly the people gathered.

The Imposter ordered, "Speak, feathers!" But the two heron feathers on the panther cap just drooped down and would not stand erect or say a word.

"They are shy," muttered the Imposter. "Sometimes they are like that. Instead, the fawn pouch shall dance for you. Dance, pouch!"

he gruffly ordered. But the fawn pouch just dangled from his belt as always. It did not move at all.

"Such shy things," grumbled the false Two Feathers.

"Here," he said, "I will smoke and make magic. I will sweeten the lodge."

He reached into the fisher-skin pouch for the pipe, but the toothed jaws of the pouch bit down hard on his wrist, so he cried out. The medicine root flew out from the pouch. The real Two Feathers saw it and grabbed it up, an old man picking up an old withered stick. The Imposter gripped the pipe he had pulled from the pouch. "I forgot to tell my magic pouch it need not stand on guard," he mumbled, shaking his wrist in pain. "Silly of me. It is a powerful guardian."

He filled the pipe with tobacco. He said, "Fly, feathers, get me a coal." The feathers drooped lower. The Imposter went and put a coal to his pipe. He puffed. The bear on the pipe grimaced. The snakes coiled low and slithered into their holes. A stench and a stink rose from the pipe.

"Stop!" shouted the people, coughing, their eyes tearing with the foul smell. A cloud of smoke filled the lodge. "Put out your horrid pipe!"

Shamefaced, the Imposter put out his pipe.

The real Two Feathers called hoarsely, "I have something good for you. Let me have a bowl." His wife handed him a wooden bowl.

Two Feathers took the medicine root. He chewed the dark end.

He blew into the bowl. The bowl filled with dark, smooth wampum beads.

"Ah!" exclaimed the people, drawing close.

"I need another bowl," said Two Feathers. A woman immediately handed one to him. He chewed the light end of the root. He blew into the bowl. White wampum filled the bowl.

"AH!" exclaimed the people with one breath. That old, useless man had just produced a great deal of treasure!

"I thought my daughter knew her mind," smiled the chief. "Son-in-Law," he said, looking curiously at Two Feathers, "whoever you are, you are a great man."

The Imposter said, "Bah, anyone can do it. Bring a bowl." His wife handed him a bowl. He spit into it. Dark shiny things piled there. "See," he said smugly. But the dark things began to move. They were bugs!

"Ugh!" exclaimed the people, pulling away.

"Bring another bowl," shouted the Imposter. At last someone reluctantly handed him an old cracked bowl. He held it to his mouth and spit into it. "Ah!" exclaimed the people excitedly. For when he held it out, it seemed to be filled with white wampum beads. But the beads began to move. They uncoiled. It was a bowl of tiny white worms.

"UGH!" exclaimed the people, drawing away. The women angrily took their fouled bowls, emptied them outside, and scrubbed them clean.

The Imposter went to the alcove of his wife. All night he lay there as he had the night before, refusing to remove his beautiful clothes. Without those clothes his wife would see him as he really was. He was afraid too that the real Two Feathers would steal those clothes back if he ever took them off. Then all the people would see what he really was.

In the morning Two Feathers said hoarsely, in his old, cracked voice, "Let us have a hunting contest. Let the two new husbands compete."

The Imposter said, "Ridiculous! How can this old fool compete against a strong young man like me?!"

"Are you afraid?" asked Two Feathers.

"Of course not!" shouted the Imposter. "I lost my bow." Someone handed him a bow and a quiver of arrows. He left the village, hunting.

Two Feathers raised his old, crooked bow and set an arrow to the string. "Deer," he said. He shot. The arrow sped away. The people looked at one another. They heard a loud crashing from among the trees. Four deer came running, crashing out from the underbrush among the trees. They stopped before Two Feathers. The arrow came following after. It struck all four deer, who tumbled down dead. Two Feathers knelt down, offering prayers for their lives. "Thank you for your gift of life," he said. The people were astonished and amazed. That old man was no burden after all, but a treasure-bringer and a hunter with magical powers!

Later that day the Imposter returned, an old, smelly fox draped over his shoulders. "See what I have brought!" he exclaimed proudly. But the people just laughed at him.

They feasted that night, and even the Imposter ate his fill. So full was he that he lay bloated on his bed. He took off the beautiful clothes, now torn and dirtied, greasy and frayed, dropping them in a disorderly pile. Then he lay back, snoring.

Turkey heard those snores. He flapped down from his shelf. He went to the Imposter's alcove. He took up the good clothes and brought them to Two Feathers. Two Feathers stripped off the old man's clothes and put on his own panther shirt. He put on the wild-cat leggings and the moccasins and the fisher pouch. He put on the fawn-skin pouch with the dangling hoofs. At once Two Feathers became young again. He was strong and handsome. At once his clothes too became new. His wife smiled and said, "Welcome, my husband. Welcome, to the real Two Feathers."

Two Feathers stood before the people. "I am Two Feathers," he said, "in my own true form once more."

The people looked at him, dazed. "Can it be?" they asked one another.

"Will you tell them, feathers?" asked Two Feathers. The two heron feathers stood straight up on his panther cap and exclaimed, "This is the real Two Feathers."

"Will you dance, my pouch?" asked Two Feathers. The fawn-skin pouch dropped from his belt and turned into a little fawn, which danced and leaped and skipped around the lodge. Then it jumped back onto his belt and hung there, just a pouch again.

"I will smoke," said Two Feathers. The fisher pouch opened its mouth, and Two Feathers reached in and took out his pipe and tobacco. The two feathers turned into birds. They flew to the fire, and each brought a coal. Two Feathers lit his pipe. The bear's eyes on the pipe lit up. The bear opened its mouth wide in a grin and growled. The snakes on the pipe slithered and hissed. A sweet odor filled the lodge, cleansing and freshening.

The people exclaimed, "You *are* the real Two Feathers!"

The Imposter's wife gave a shriek. There, in her bed, lay an old, filthy, wrinkled man. The Imposter looked up groggily. He saw the horrified expression on his young wife's face. He hopped down from the bed, grabbed his old clothes, flung them on, and leaped out the door of the lodge. He ran off into the woods and was never seen again.

Turkey and Two Feathers lived for a time in that village.

One day, Two Feathers and Turkey announced that they must go back to their old uncle, who lived all alone in an old lodge and who needed their help. The chief said, "We will go with you. We shall live where you live, all together."

Then they traveled back. It was a long way and took quite some time. How glad the old uncle was to see his nephews once again! He knew, seeing them safe and well and grown, that many sorrows were gone from the world and that the sorcerers who lay in wait to bring harm had been overcome at last. Yes, how proud he was, how happy to have them back. And how glad he was too, that Two Feathers's wife was so kind, clearheaded, and such a good cook too!

The old lodge was repaired, and many new ones built. The village prospers still. If you go there, you will find it. So the story goes."

The Stone paused. "So it is," it said, "that happy endings come at last. But patience is needed. Good wins in the end, and the Imposter is always unmasked. But it may take a long time, and many seemingly unjust things can happen along the way."

The men nodded, thinking of the difficult things they had each seen. Crow was quiet, thinking of his mother, father, and sister. Even the usually merry Raccoon seemed subdued.

The Stone said, "Isn't that right, Fist?"

Fist looked up, fear in his eyes. He looked wildly at his brother, Two Arrows, then at the others. He half-stood as if to run or grab a weapon and fight, then sank back down again among the ferns, hung his head, and nodded guiltily. The other men looked at him, dismayed and confused. Two Arrows exclaimed with some fear and anger, "What is this? What have you done? What does the Stone mean? Tell us!"

"I . . . am a spy. On you! An imposter. Bear Claw sent me to join you. He has been suspicious of where you and the boys go. Maybe you plan something that brings danger to the tribe. Maybe you meet with our enemies. But . . . but I like the stories. I will tell him nothing. Let me travel this trail with you and return."

The Stone said, "There is nothing more to hide. Tell Bear Claw. Tell all the People. It is time. The stories may be heard by all now. The time for hiding is over. All shall be unmasked. Crow, tonight you shall tell the chief and all the People to come back here with you tomorrow."

"Me!" exclaimed Crow. "Who would follow me? Grandfather, you do not understand our ways. I am less than nobody. The People will laugh and mock me. None will come."

"Grandmother will come," said Raccoon.

"We will stand with you," said Eagle. All the men — even Fist — nodded. "The People will come."

The Stone said, "It grows late, I say. I shall rest now. Go back to your village with this news — if they bring gifts, they will hear stories. It is time to end my tale."

Crow's heart seemed to expand and burst bonds long tied tightly around it. The time for hiding was over. Tonight he would not have to lie again but could finally speak his truth. No longer would he be an imposter. He could at last tell Grandmother all. "Tomorrow, Grandfather," he exclaimed excitedly.

They gathered their weapons. The sky was darkening, and the air was chill. Overhead a long, wavering V of geese could be seen above the trees. Their cries, faint and poignant, came clearly to them. Soon the geese would be gone. Soon the snows would come.

Briskly they set off together. The twilight deepened. The air, clear and blue, darkened. A first star awoke, like the faint campfire of a distant, traveling people settling for the night. The forest thinned. They could smell the smoke of cooking fires. Crow paused. They all slowed their trot. "I have no food for Grandmother!" exclaimed Crow in exasperation.

"Wait," said Fist. He looked at his brother, Two Arrows, at Wolf Jaw and Eagle. The men smiled, nodded, and ran off. Raccoon and Crow waited among the trees, watching the stars gather and shimmer overhead. The Brothers danced, sparkling in the sky overhead, and while they waited, Crow pointed to them and told Raccoon the first tale that Grandfather Stone had told him, the tale of the Dancing Boys. Soon the men returned with dried meat, boiled squash, corn, and fry bread. "Take this," they said. "Eat, then join us at the lodge of Pine Tree Alone."

They parted, Raccoon and the men heading on into the village and Crow going to the old lodge. When he entered he was met by the sharp smell of pine-needle tea — a heartening, restorative drink but not very nourishing. Grandmother looked up and drew a sharp breath, sucking the air in through her teeth. "*Noh-kweh!*" she exclaimed. "What is this?" She rose heavily to her feet. "These are not birds! Who has given you this — and why?"

"I go to the lodge of Pine Tree Alone," answered Crow. "Eagle and others want me to . . . speak. They have given us food. We shall eat, then I will go."

Grandmother's eyebrows shot up. Her jaw dropped. "Eagle wants you to speak in Council, in the lodge of the old chief? Men who I . . . who I . . . they want you to . . . to speak?" she repeated in disbelief. Then she added anxiously, "But, why? Is there danger?"

"There is no danger," smiled Crow. "While we eat I will tell you some things. Then tomorrow you shall see all for yourself."

Then, while Crow and Grandmother sat together and ate, Crow told of how one day, not all that long ago and yet so far back that it seemed as if in another world, he came upon a stone, a Talking Stone. Then he told too of Grandfather Stone's Long-Ago Time stories. Now, he said, the time had come for all to hear.

"I knew that there was more to it," said Grandmother almost contentedly, "but why was your hunting so poor?"

"It was late each day when I left Grandfather, the days were growing short, and it was too dark to hunt well. And, after a time, somehow, I no longer had the heart for the killing. There is another trail that I follow. You will see. But will you come hear Grandfather Stone speak?"

"I will," said Grandmother.

The boy rose happily. "I am glad," he said. "Just wait till you hear Grandfather's stories!" Then he added anxiously, "Now I go to the Council."

THE COUNCIL

◆ ◆ ◆

CROW ran excitedly along the dark trail that led to the village. Outside the lodge of Pine Tree Alone, he paused, looked up at the Brothers dancing and shining overhead, took a deep breath, lifted the flap, and entered.

The old chief, Pine Tree Alone, raised his gray eyebrows as Crow entered. He looked calmly, yet expectantly, at the boy. The chief wore a simple breechclout. A plain deerskin cap with a single eagle feather standing upright in it was on his head, and a sash of white and purple wampum was draped across his shoulder. Others in the lodge were more grandly dressed, wearing shell earrings and necklaces, fancy embroidered deerskin leggings and moccasins. Even so, the old chief stood out. Though his long hair was gray and his face lined and creased, his one, dark eye was sensitively alert and bright. The other eye was shriveled and closed, having been torn and blinded in a raid many years before. He nodded in a friendly way to the boy and, with a large hand, motioned him forward.

Several warriors seated near Bear Claw jumped to their feet, gesturing angrily. Then Eagle stood up and boldly announced, "This boy is a messenger, with a powerful spirit as his guide. I have met it, as have others." He motioned at Wolf Jaw and Two Arrows, who rose and stood at his shoulders. Fist rose and walked from his place near Bear Claw to stand beside his older brother and the others. Bear Claw's face flushed and twisted with anger. Raccoon peered bright-eyed from behind his father's shoulder.

"Speak, child," said Pine Tree Alone.

Crow said, "I have listened to Grandfather Stone. He asks that you come. Bring gifts and —"

The warriors who had leaped up at Crow's entrance now interrupted, exclaiming, "Cast out the orphan! He brings bad luck! His grandmother is a witch! Who is he, an outcast boy who lives with a grandmother, to speak to men?"

Eagle and the others cried, "Shame!" Eagle added, "This boy is young, poor, and orphaned, it is true. But he has a man's heart. The earth speaks to him. We have heard it. His grandmother is an old woman. She has suffered. Does this make her a witch? You say you are grown men. Bah! You prattle like children! Let the boy speak! He has man's words, not those of a child."

The old chief still looked steadily at Crow. The rising hubbub had not touched him at all. Waves of strife could break against him, but he would remain solid, considering, thinking of what was best for his People. So it was now. "Let the orphan speak," he said calmly. "His father, Ga'no, gave thoughtful counsel. He was truthful and brave. Speak, child."

Crow took a breath and said, "Grandfather Stone has sent me. He says you may come. Bring gifts. In exchange, you will hear Long-Ago Time tales — stories of the world before this one."

Then Bear Claw leaped to his feet, a polished bear claw necklace rattling at his throat. His face was hard, chiseled as a spear blade. The scars on his chest attested to his ferocity in battle. He sneered venomously at Crow and stared murderously at Fist. Then he said, "'The world before this one'! And what is that? Child's talk! Here is the real world — the world of men and battles and the tribe's survival. And in this real world I do not follow *boys*. We, who are *men*, lead, and do not follow. Let him starve. But, if he is strong enough, he will live. Maybe, then, he will be of use to the People."

"Hunh," muttered several men, nodding in agreement.

Then Bear Claw smiled. "Perhaps the old woman uses the boy to regain a place among us," he said. "An old woman's trick. I say again — the weak are not needed. We must be strong to destroy our foes!" He shook his balled war club with its flint spike to emphasize his stern point.

Pine Tree Alone nodded, saying, "Bear Claw is a great warrior and speaks well. His words clearly carry only the good of the People out from his strong heart."

Many nodded now, agreeing, confirming these supportive words. Bear Claw looked around at the men of the Council proudly. Eagle, Wolf Jaw, Two Arrows, and Fist glanced darkly at one another.

"Still," continued the old chief, squinting his one good eye as if turning its light within, "we all must agree that Gaqka's father, Ga'no — Arrow — was also both truthful and brave. What harm can there be in following his son a few steps into the forest and finding out the truth for ourselves? I say we should examine carefully what has been presented to us. I say we should come."

There was silence as the men chewed on the chief's words. The fire flickered. Bear Claw scowled. Then he shrugged and said, "What harm can it be? A waste of time, maybe. A trap. I, for one, will go well-armed. But if the boy is simply wrong or lying, so be it. He will starve or live by his own strength. If he lies, we will all know his falsehood. It will be clear, and I will be content. It is one to me. The good of the People is my only concern."

Pine Tree Alone nodded. "We will come," he said to Crow.

The Council was over.

Dawn came, and Crow awoke. From a bark box Grandmother lifted a pair of moccasins, embroidered with porcupine quills.

"Today, Grandson," she said, "these are for you." She handed Crow the moccasins. "I prepared them for the day you would be honored as a fine hunter. But put them on today. This is your day."

Crow took the moccasins, admiring the quillwork design of

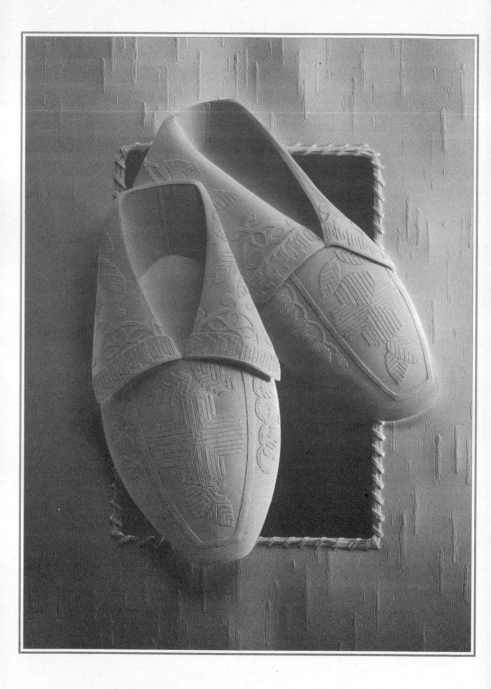

trees, stems, leaves, and flowers. "With these on, Grandmother," he said, "even in winter I walk on flowers."

"What a talker you are," laughed Grandmother.

Laughing too, he put on the new moccasins.

"I want to hear Long-Ago Time stories," said Grandmother seriously. "I want to hear tales of the world before this one. Wear them when you tell the stories the Stone told you. I think now that you will tell them."

They went out together. Coming toward their little broken-down lodge with its cracked bark roof and walls was a line of people carrying gifts. Pine Tree Alone walked at the front of the line and he welcomed Crow and Grandmother. "Walk here, beside me," he said to Crow.

THE PEOPLE
AND THE STONE

◆ ◆ ◆

THEN the People set out together in a long line, winding along the trail, Crow walking beside the chief, Pine Tree Alone. At last they came to the clearing. It had taken a good while, for they had moved no faster than Grandmother could hobble. The sun was high above the trees.

The People entered the clearing and surrounded the Stone. They cut the brush away and bent branches, so there would be room for all. They offered gifts of many kinds — flint knives and axes; corn, beans, and squash; rattles and baskets, shells and freshwater pearls, hickory bows, red willow arrows, embroidered moccasins and shirts, turkey-wing fans, eagle feathers; chunks of fry bread and maple sugar, dried deer meat, pouches of tobacco and sunflower seeds. Crow set down his bow, his quiver of arrows, and his one old moccasin.

When all had given their gifts and were seated, Grandfather

Stone at last spoke. "*Dadjoh,*" it said. "Welcome. Do not be afraid. I live and am very old. I wish no harm but only good, so be at ease. I am glad you have come. Soon I will rest. The time is nearing in which I can be silent again. But you have come to hear stories, so listen —"

But before Grandfather Stone could say another word, a voice shouted, "*Weyoh!* It is true! Ha! Ha ha! Oh ho, such poor spies!"

Crow and all the people watched, amazed, as Grandmother leaped to her feet and did a little dance. "The boy said it!" she whooped. "But now I see! Now I hear! Now it is so! My spies were such poor spies!"

Raccoon, Eagle, Blossoms Falling, Two Feathers, Fist, and Wolf Jaw joined with her, laughing heartily. Soon all the people, when they heard the tale of Grandmother's spies, joined in. Moons Walking laughed along with Willows Talk and little Flowers Playing. The young warriors laughed, as did the old chief, Pine Tree Alone. Only Bear Claw managed to refrain from bursting out laughing. His own spy had failed him too. But the Stone really did speak. So far, at least that much was true. He watched all that happened warily still. When the general merriment subsided and all had ceased wiping tears of glee from their eyes, Grandfather Stone began again.

"Yes," it chuckled, "you were right, Grandmother. Early on you caught the scent of our little game. But only now did the time become ripe to reveal it. Now that you are here at last," continued the Stone, "there are ways you must know. This is how it shall be.

When a storyteller announces that a story will be told, you must respond, '*Nio!*' If the teller pauses and does not go on, he or she shall be testing to see if you follow, and you must say, '*He!*' to show that you listen. Stay alert! Listen well until the words '*Da neho nig aga is*' — 'Now the story is finished.' Or, '*Neh-hoh*' — 'It is done.' This is how it shall be from now on. This is the way it has always been in worlds before this one." Then the Stone was silent.

"*He!*" said the old chief and the people.

"There was a boy," began the Stone. "He was young, no more than seven or eight. He was hunting birds, for he was too small to hunt larger creatures, and was standing beside a small river watching the treetops, listening carefully, when he heard a sound — *swish, swish*. He looked upstream. There, coming around a bend in the river, was a tiny canoe no longer than a man's forearm. And in that canoe were two tiny men paddling hard, moving along at a rapid pace. The boy was astonished.

The tiny men stopped the canoe at the boy's feet. They looked up to where he towered like a giant above them. They looked at his bow and arrows — huge weapons to them. One of the men asked in a high little voice, "Will you trade your fine bow and arrows with us?" He pointed to his own weapons, a tiny quiver of tiny but perfect arrows and a bow of matching size.

The boy looked at his own bow, at his own arrows. For the first time he saw how large and powerful they were. He felt pride. He smiled and shook his head. "No," he said. "Your weapons are too small for me. I could not shoot anything with them. They would be toys."

The little man shook his head sadly from side to side. He lifted his bow, slipped an arrow from the quiver, drew the string back, pointed the tiny bow skyward, and shot. The arrow leaped up higher and higher and higher and higher until it was a mere speck in the sky. Continuing on ever higher and higher, it was soon gone from sight.

"Small things must never be discounted," said the little man. "There is power in everything. Sometimes it is greatest, because most concentrated, in the very small. What is the invisible world but the smallest of all, so small it is unseen, yet is it not the most powerful?"

Then the two men lifted their paddles and shot rapidly away. In less than a minute they were gone.

The boy ran back to the lodge where he lived with his grandmother.

"Grandmother!" he exclaimed excitedly. "I met small men in a tiny canoe. They wanted my bow and arrows and would have given me one of their bows and a quiver of tiny arrows in exchange. I would not trade. Their weapons seemed like babies' toys. But I learned about power. Their tiny bows were mightier than any bow I have ever seen, more powerful than any drawn by even the most mighty warrior."

His grandmother shook her head and smiled ruefully. "You have met the *Djo-geh-onh*, the Little People. Some of these small ones

181

live underground and keep *otgont* creatures from emerging onto the surface world and causing harm. Some live among the plants and help them grow. Some dwell among flowing streams and can change the shape of the surface world, bring down trees, move boulders. Alas, that you did not take their gift. No bow shoots farther or more accurately than theirs. No arrow is swifter.

"Learn from this. As you grow, never think to look down on others. No matter how humble or small they may be, you never know the wisdom or power they may carry within. Never forget this. Let it be a lesson that lasts your whole life."

The boy took it to heart and never forgot those good words. So I say to you, never disregard the young or the small. There is good power in everything. Some of you may have doubted the wisdom of following a child. But I say you have done well to overcome your doubts and follow. It will be to your benefit and to the benefit of your People not only now, but for generations. Out of small things may come much that is of value.

"Now you too will know stories of this world and the world before this. I speak for the Earth Mother, she who woke me from my sleep. She has had enough of your bickering, your wars and raids, of your taking of life without the giving of prayer. The time has come for you too to wake up and live again in a sacred manner. It is time. I shall tell another story."

"*Nio!*" exclaimed the people, even Bear Claw joining in.

"It was like this," began the Stone. "Long ago Chipmunk was

out hurrying around, finding seeds and acorns, stuffing his pouches and storing what he could. Bear saw him and, with a great swipe of one huge paw, pinned him down.

"I am hungry," said Bear slowly. "You will be a tasty morsel. I shall eat you now."

"No, no!" desperately squeaked Chipmunk. "Don't eat me yet. Let me dance first. Let me show you the dance of the chipmunks. It is very old and powerful."

"Powerful!" laughed Bear gruffly. "Ho ho! I am powerful. You are the tiniest of creatures. I see no power in you."

"Let me dance!" squeaked Chipmunk. "You will like it. What harm can it do? You will soon eat me anyway."

"I will," agreed Bear. "Yes, I will. Well, then, dance!" And he lifted his great paw.

Chipmunk sneezed and rose from the dust. He cleaned his fur and rubbed his nose. Then he began to dance. He danced and danced, pounding on the leaves with all his strength.

Bear watched in delight, swaying to the rhythm of Chipmunk's dance.

As Chipmunk stamped he was feeling with his tiny feet under the leaves. He danced and danced all around until he thought he felt a soft spot, a tunnel entrance under the leaves. Carefully, carefully he pounded there more and more insistently until yes! yes! he was sure. There was a small hole! With a sudden turn and a great leap he jumped straight down into the hole beneath the leaves.

Bear reached out swiftly with a great paw to catch him. The claws raked down along Chipmunk's neck and back as down the hole he tumbled. Then down the corridors of the old mouse den Chipmunk safely ran. He had escaped.

In time the wounds scabbed over. When they healed, dark lines were left on Chipmunk's neck and back for all to see. So all chipmunks are marked to this day."

"So," said the Stone when the people's laughter had ceased. "I see you liked that tale. Chipmunk's stripes show Bear's power. Yet they show too that little Chipmunk had the power to outsmart the mighty Bear. He had power of his own after all."

Then Grandfather Stone told stories throughout that day, tales of the Long-Ago Time, of the past now long forgotten.

Late in the afternoon the Stone paused. "It is time to rest," it said. "You have listened well. It grows dark, and cold night comes. Return tomorrow. I will tell more."

Then the old chief, Pine Tree Alone, rose and thanked Grandfather Stone. The people rose and offered thanks too. Then, following the chief, Crow, and Grandmother, they all returned to the village.

That night people came to Crow and Grandmother's lodge with food and gifts. Moons Walking and Willows Talk brought a deerskin. Flowers Playing brought a deerskin pouch. "I made this for you," she said to Crow. "You can't drop it. See — the thong slips over your neck. And see? It closes tight, so nothing can fall out. Not even moccasins."

Her father, the stern warrior Bear Claw, came too. "Here, boy," he said gruffly, holding out a deer haunch. "Eat and grow strong. The People might have use for you after all." He nodded and left.

There was so much food, it was more like a feast than a meal. Crow sat somewhat shamefaced beside the fire. The attention was embarrassing!

Eagle and Blossoms Falling, Wolf Jaw, Two Arrows and Raccoon brought food too.

"Stay, spies," insisted Grandmother. "Eat with us."

"Grandmother, you were right," said Eagle when they were seated. "There was a secret, but it was not *otgont* — as you now see." He broke off a piece of fry bread, scooped up some boiled squash and venison stew, and munched happily. "And it was a hard secret, I think," he added between mouthfuls, "for Gaqka to keep too."

Raccoon agreed. "Just look at him now. How shamefaced he looks!"

"I couldn't tell you," Crow said. "I wanted to, but Grandfather Stone said I wasn't ready."

Grandmother looked as if she was about to scold. Then she laughed. "But now you are. I am glad to know my suspicions were true. At least I have not yet entirely lost my wits! It worked out well, making a story with a good ending!"

Then Crow and Grandmother, Eagle, Blossoms Falling, Raccoon, Wolf Jaw, Two Arrows, and Fist ate together, laughing and talking in the old lodge at the edge of the village, where the forest began.

For the next three days the people came to Grandfather Stone with gifts. For three days the Stone spoke. On the fourth day the Stone said, "We each have a choice. Even I. Narrow dreams destroy. But some dreams give life. Many changes are to happen, some things beyond belief. I can see down the trail ahead. A little bit I can see of what is to come, and it is impossible to describe even this tiny bit. Yet the truths of these stories will never change, no matter what may come. Dreaming well, acting with kindness toward all, no, this can never be exhausted or outgrown. As long as grass grows and rivers flow, the good truths of these stories will endure.

"That is all," said the Stone. "There is nothing more to say. It is finished. Remember the stories. Tell them when the frosts begin and when the snows blanket the sleeping hills. That is the time for stories, when the tasks of growing and gathering are done and the forest, birds, plants, and animals sleep. Hearing the stories you will be renewed and readied again for the quickening of spring. I have done what I can. Now I shall rest. If you want to hear more tales, speak to the boy, speak to Gaqka. He knows tales. Ask him. He will tell them to you. He is a *Ha-ge-o-tah*, a storyteller, a teller of the tales of the Long-Ago Time. There will be others. He is the first in this world, in this time."

All thanked Grandfather Stone. Then thoughtfully, led by the old chief, they returned to the village.

That night the old chief called for a runner. "Go to our foes," he said. "There has been enough killing. We shall meet with them and see if there is a way to bring peace. Let us bury our weapons together at last."

That night Crow said to Grandmother, "We have a place among the People now. But let us stay in this old lodge. We will have food enough. I will tell stories. Staying here, close to the forest, will help me remember. I do not want to live amidst the bustle and chatter of the village. I will stay here, near the trees, birds, and animals."

Surprised, Grandmother answered, "Maybe later you will change your mind."

"I do not think so," answered Crow, in a voice very much like that of Ga'no, his father. "When I am older and, perhaps, have a family of my own, even then, I think, I will live here. I will repair this old lodge, and, if need arises, make it big enough for those yet to come."

FAREWELL

♦ ♦ ♦

THE next morning Crow returned alone to the glade. The sky was low, the clouds yellowish-gray. A light rain was falling.

Crow called to Grandfather Stone, but there was no answer. He walked closer. On top of Grandfather Stone was a small black rock — shaped like a crow! Yes. There was the beak, the wing, the balancing tail. It was his namesake, Crow the Talker, the teller of *gaa! gaa!* Of stories!

Rain pattered on the leafy ground and gathered in pools on the back of Grandfather Stone, streaking the glittering, veined surface in dark wet lines. A glossy black shadow glided overhead. Two more crows flew closer and perched nearby. Bobbing their heads, they peered down at the boy.

"Thank you, Grandfather," whispered Crow, lifting the crow-stone. "I gave you my weapons. I will not kill again. I gave you

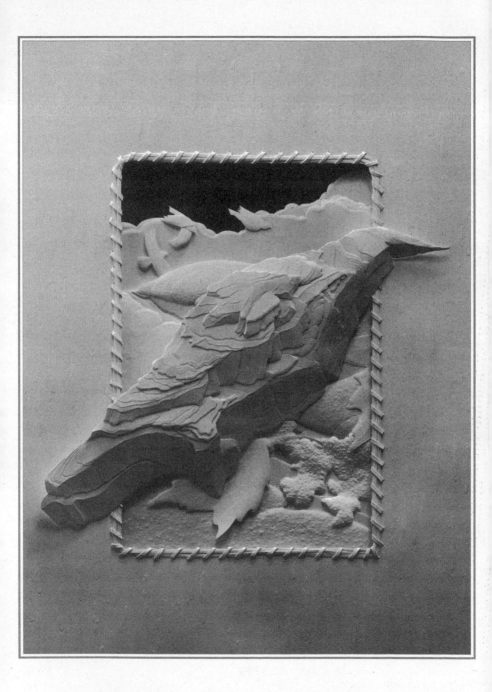

my moccasin, for I am no longer a child. I will feed the People, but not with meat. Thank you for all your gifts. Sleep well." He placed his hand on the cold, wet, mossy surface of Grandfather Stone. Snow began to fall, just a few flakes swirling down in the light, cool rain.

With a chuckling, insistent *Gaa! Gaa!* the watching crows flapped their wings, rose up, and flew off, circling the glade before disappearing beyond the trees.

Crow watched until they were just specks, until they were gone. Then he too set off back to the old lodge at the edge of the forest, back home.

That night a messenger came requesting that the *Ha-ge-o-tah*, Gaqka — Crow — come to the lodge of the chief, Pine Tree Alone, and tell tales. So Crow and Grandmother went, Crow wearing his new moccasins and carrying in the deerskin pouch the crow-stone and a pinch of corn pollen. Solemnly, he took his place by the fire, Grandmother seated proudly nearby. Gifts were placed before him.

Then Crow said, "I will tell a Long-Ago Time tale."

"*Nio!*" exclaimed the gathered people.

"Long long ago," began Crow, "in a time so far back it is beyond all knowing, all remembering, there was a chief of the Sky World who lived with his young and beauteous bride." He paused. The flames of the fire crackled in the sudden silence.

"*He!*" exclaimed the people.

Crow smiled at Grandmother. He nodded his head and looked across the fire at all who were gathered, expectantly waiting. He took a breath, and then he told the whole marvelous tale of the Creation, which his own teacher, the Storytelling Stone, had told to him so long ago, back in a world before this one.

AUTHOR'S NOTE

❖ ❖ ❖   *The World Before This One* is a book of Seneca tales woven together
to form one long story about memory, storytelling, and the role of stories in
our lives and communities. The novelistic framing tale that contains all the
others — the story of the boy named Crow, who is told stories of the world
before this one by a Boulder — was also inspired by a traditional Seneca
legend.

The Seneca are one of the founding nations of the mighty Iroquois
Confederacy, or Great League of Peace, formed around 1450 c.e. The other
nations of that great union — which was a model for the political union of the
thirteen original colonies into the United States — are the Mohawk, Oneida,
Onondaga, and Cayuga (and later the Tuscarora), establishing the Five and
later Six Nations.

Two strong, brief, and quite different versions of our central tale of the boy,
the Boulder, and the origin of stories may be easily found. One is in Arthur
Parker's venerable *Seneca Myths and Folk Tales,* the other in Jeremiah Curtin's
Seneca Indian Myths. Both are classic works and were vital sources for this
book. Jesse Cornplanter's well-known and important *Legends of the Longhouse*, Arthur Parker's *Skunny Wundy: Seneca Indian Tales*, Tehanetorens's

Tales of the Iroquois, and E. A. Smith's *Myths of the Iroquois* were also valuable sources. Versions of stories inspired by these works appear in *The World Before This One* as well. Those interested in Iroquois storytelling in general and in Seneca tales in particular will find a wealth of valuable information and many wonderful stories in these books. Readers should be aware that, as is usual in oral traditions, different, equally genuine tellings of any one tale may exist. Each reflects the vision, knowledge, and narrative skill of an individual storyteller. Any one version is not necessarily "truer" or more real. As Grandfather Stone might have said to Crow, "All versions taken together come closest to the truth."

The particular stories selected for *The World Before This One* do not present a traditional cycle of tales. But, in recreating and reweaving them, I found that they did have a unifying theme.

Having lived for thirty years in Rochester, New York, at the traditional Western Door of the Great Longhouse of the Haudenosaunee — the Iroquois, the People of the Longhouse — I have had the good fortune to hike, canoe, camp, kayak, and motorcycle through what was all, once, Seneca land. Ganandagan, the New York State Historic and Sacred Seneca site, has also generously given me the opportunity to tell stories in the context of the old ways — on a winter's night, before a fire, and within an actual longhouse. *The World Before This One* reflects these experiences, even as its stories embody the unique life of this place. May it serve as a small offering toward the debt of gratitude we all owe the Seneca People, whose long tradition of generosity, political savvy, sophisticated ecological awareness, and spiritual wisdom form one of the great treasures, not just of New York State, and these United States, but of the world.

The story of the boy, Crow, who hears stories from a Talking Stone, also has some special, personal import for me. As a child growing up in New York City, a boulder was one of my own earliest companions. The boulder had been deposited when the glaciers melted and retreated, more than ten thousand years ago. When I climbed up on it, it spoke, telling me tales of times that had been before the city reared itself over the land. My boulder had seen woolly mammoths, pristine forests, and sparkling rivers. It had known the first peoples and their children. In summer, it radiated back the sun's own warmth. Like Crow's Grandfather Stone, it lived and told tales.

Alas, my storytelling boulder has long since been bulldozed away. But the earth beneath our feet remains a real, living Storytelling Stone, one that knows all the tales of the worlds before this one.

RAFE MARTIN
March 2002

A spell turns Ardwin's arm into a wing. Is it a blessing—or a curse?

Instead of a left arm, Prince Ardwin has an enchanted wing. Can Ardwin—half bird, half boy— ever find his place in the world? Or will his very existence spark a devastating war?

■ SCHOLASTIC

SCHOLASTIC and associated logos are trademarks and/or registered trademarks of Scholastic Inc.   BRDWT